The Devil Inside

Barb Jones

Immortal Cravings LLC.

Copyright © 2026 by Barb Jones.

All rights reserved.

Library of Congress Number (LCCN): 2025927577

ISBN (Paperback): 979-8-9922349-5-4

Publisher: Immortal Cravings, LLC

Editor: Paige Lawson

Cover Designer: Brandi Kae Designs

This is a work of fiction. Names, characters, places, and incidents are products of the author's imagination or are used fictitiously and are not to be construed as real. Any resemblance to actual events, locations, organizations, living or dead persons is entirely coincidental.

DEDICATION

This book is dedicated to Cheryl Ridgeway and her husband, Dennis. Thank you for designing this cover and helping me to bring H.H. Holmes to life again.

Contents

Prologue	1
1. The Child	6
2. The Cabin	13
3. The Slow Grip	21
4. The First Night	28
5. Harold's Ledger	34
6. Harold's Pursuit	42
7. The Heart of the House	49
8. The Forest and the Ledger	56
9. Inheritance	64
10. The Bone Ledger	76
11. The Inheritance of Echoes	84
12. The Aftermath	92
13. Hollow Point	103
14. The Ledger Beneath	116
15. The Quiet Between Pages	129

16. The Sound After Silence	138
17. Margins That Still Bleed	145
18. Revision	152
19. Resurrection Draft	160
20. PUBLICATION	166
21. Syndication	173
22. The Residuals	180
23. The Revision Ritual	187
24. The Final Draft	194
Epilogue	200
About The Author	203
Other Works	205

Prologue

Murder Castle, December 24th, 1891 — Englewood, Chicago

Gaslight burned low, its flame breathing in rhythm with the pulse beneath her ribs. The walls of the operating room gleamed like bone, white tile catching the lamp's uneven quiver. Instruments waited on a steel tray—scalpels, clamps, glass syringes—each polished until it reflected her face in thin, ghostly slices.

The air smelled of phenol and metal, sharp enough to sting the back of her throat. Chicago never smelled this clean, she thought. The city's scents were a living confusion—coal smoke and horse, bakery steam and snow. Noise you could breathe. But here, the air was sterilized of memory. No dust. No kindness.

She remembered Clark Street at noon: laughter, barkers, the tobacconist who tipped his hat. And Holmes—tilting his head just so, listening with the courteous stillness that made her feel chosen, as if the whole world had hushed for her alone. In that hush, she had mistaken being seen for being safe.

Somewhere beyond the door, footsteps passed and faded. The room had no windows, only the hiss of gas through pipes, a mechanical heartbeat that refused to stop.

Julia opened her eyes to find her lover drawing on a pair of gloves. Months had passed since she'd come to work for him, since admiration had blurred into love. He had been patient, soft-spoken, unfailingly gentle. Today, when she'd told him she was with child, he'd promised marriage—after "the inconvenience" was handled. His persuasion had been smooth as the gloves he wore now.

Her thoughts clung to her daughter. Pearl was all that tethered her to the world as Holmes prepared the instruments. He spoke softly, almost lovingly, as he adjusted the burner's flame. "You must trust me, dearest. I've delivered women from far worse burdens than yours."

She scarcely heard him over the racing of her heart. The first cut drew a cry she didn't know she could make. He didn't flinch. When she screamed again, he laughed—low, deliberate—as his fingers twirled the ends of his moustache. The man she had loved had vanished. In his place stood a craftsman of cruelty.

Blood slicked her lips. "Pearl," she whispered.

Holmes paused, smiling faintly. "We discussed this," he said gently, as if soothing a nervous patient. "A child born of sin would ruin us both. You'll recover soon, and then we'll be wed. We'll start again, clean."

He turned to the beaker, the gas hissing louder. The smell of antiseptic filled the room. He hummed under his breath—a tuneless sound she had once found endearing. Now it curdled her blood.

She watched the profile she had once memorized—the symmetry that had fooled her, the composure of a man who believed the world existed for dissection. Even his affection had been clinical. He loved order, even in sin. Each smile, each word had been an experiment designed to test her devotion.

The lamp flickered. Shadows rearranged themselves across the walls. The instruments' reflections lengthened like knives cut from moonlight. In the wavering light she saw other rooms layered over this one—Pearl in her nightdress, Ned's hat on its peg, the stairwell of their home breathing in the winter cold. All of them overlapping, folding inward. The pipes hummed through it all, steady as a metronome counting down the distance to silence.

She thought of home: the smell of bread on Sundays, Ned's gentle voice. He had never deserved betrayal. She had only wanted to be loved differently. Holmes had offered her escape, and she had mistaken curiosity for care. He had studied her despair the way other men studied anatomy.

Consciousness frayed. Memories blurred. Pearl's laughter in the kitchen; sugar dust on small hands. The first snow, the promise of marriage, the way Holmes's eyes gleamed when she said yes.

Pain roared back. "Pearl," she gasped again. "Where is my Pearl?"

Holmes's voice remained calm. "She's with friends, safe from worry. She'll come once we've finished here."

The truth struck colder than the tile beneath her skin. He meant to kill them both. Fury cut through fear. She spat at him, though blood blurred her aim. "End it, and be damned."

His mask cracked. The next incision was savage. "The womb contracts even now," he murmured to himself, voice clinical. "Remarkable."

She stopped listening. Breath came in ragged bursts, the edges of her vision narrowing. Above her, the ceiling pulsed with light, then dimmed. She felt her soul begin to loosen. But before the dark could claim her, she found her voice.

"Before death claims my soul," she whispered, "I curse you to wander in purgatory. Your torment shall be my redemption. May Heaven send an angel to cast you into Hell when your suffering is complete."

Her lips cracked; blood slicked her teeth. Yet the air around her trembled. The gaslight wavered. Something unseen passed through the room—a breath not her own.

The beaker shattered. Holmes stepped back, startled. For the first time, fear crossed his face. "Julia..."

She smiled, a terrible serenity in her dying eyes. "The Castle will remember me."

Then her body went still.

Holmes removed his gloves with surgical precision. He washed his hands in a basin of clear water, humming to steady himself. The blood spiraled down the drain—red, pink, gone. When he looked into the basin, his reflection quivered. Behind his eyes, another face moved—a woman's mouth forming silent words.

He staggered back, pressing a hand to his chest. The air had grown colder.

Shadows bent. The flame drew long and thin, blue as a blade. The walls seemed to breathe.

Holmes exhaled sharply, composing himself. "Nerves," he muttered. "Only nerves."

He turned to leave, adjusting his cufflinks. The door bolt clicked. His footsteps receded down the corridor—measured, deliberate, as if he still controlled the rhythm of the world.

Behind him, the room began to breathe. Condensation formed on the basin, though the water had cooled.

Across its curve, faint words appeared in fog:

I remain.

Pearl.

The letters faded as the lamp hissed low.

Holmes paused in the corridor. For a heartbeat, he thought he heard humming—soft, tuneless, a woman's voice winding through the gaslight. He turned. Nothing. Only silence, and the flicker of flame.

He continued down the hall, but his shadow lagged half a step behind, its mouth open in a silent scream he would never hear.

Back in the room, the instruments trembled as though brushed by unseen hands. The scalpel rolled once across the tray and stopped, its point aimed toward the door.

Somewhere deep in the walls, the gas line's hum shifted, low and steady, until it resembled breathing.

The Murder Castle slept.

And in its sleep, it learned to dream her name.

1
THE CHILD

The morning at the cabin smelled of pancakes and damp pine. Steam fogged the tiny window above the table while Julie counted bubbles in the batter the way her mother counted data points in a chart. Her father whistled through his teeth—off-key, cheerful—the sound of a man trying to convince the day to be kind.

"You'll scare off the birds," her mother said, but she smiled when she said it.

Julie grinned and brushed crumbs from her notebook. Inside, she'd sketched two grasshoppers sparring, their hind legs lifted like fencers. "I'm going to find one with blue wings today," she said. "They hide near the stream."

"Only if you're back before dark," her father said, pouring a careful ribbon of batter. "The woods look friendly until the sun remembers to leave."

"It's barely noon, Dad."

"Still. Woods have long shadows."

She rolled her eyes—thirteen, certain of immortality. "You and Mom worry too much."

They ate with the door propped open, letting in the sweet rot of last year's leaves. The cabin had a way of collecting morning: honey light in the dust, the crack of butter in the pan, her mother humming an unfinished hymn. Her parents fit together in small movements—her father handing her mother the plate without looking, her mother reaching for his coffee just as he thought to pour it. Julie studied them like a scientist watching a stable ecosystem: two adults pretending the world was predictable.

"Are we still going into town tomorrow?" she asked.

"Depends," Frank said. "On whether you can beat your mother at Scrabble tonight."

Leslie laughed. "Unfair advantage. He knows I hate words longer than four letters before breakfast."

Julie scribbled a note in the margin of her sketchbook: **Note—**parents simulate normalcy through humor. Then, to hide her smile, she flipped the page and drew the window: the world beyond it layered in mist and pine, the trees exhaling slow.

They'd moved here three months ago—a sabbatical, her mother called it. Time away from the city's noise, from too much knowing. Julie liked the idea that quiet could reset things. The forest made her feel small in the right way. Safe, almost. But sometimes at night, when the wind slipped between the boards, she imagined the trees whispering her name back to her. She never told her parents that part.

The smell of syrup and rain blurred until she couldn't tell which belonged inside. When breakfast ended, she lingered in the doorway, watching her parents move through the quiet choreography of dishes and talk. The cabin smelled like maple and old timber—childhood distilled.

When she pushed through the screen, the door gave its familiar squeal—summer's hinge. Air wrapped around her—green, humid, alive. The path behind the cabin still showed her boot prints from yesterday's hunt, already softened by dew.

She loved the quiet between sounds—the pause after a birdcall when the air waited to see if the forest would answer. She crouched to study a beetle climbing a fern stem, its shell flashing copper where sun pierced the canopy. Its movement soothed her: deliberate, unaware of watchers.

The ground sloped toward the stream. Ferns brushed her knees; the smell shifted from pine to iron and moss. She carried a jar in her satchel for water insects, but when she knelt at the bank, the surface looked strangely dense, as though the stream were holding its hush.

She stilled, listening. The forest answered with a vibration—low, steady, rhythmic. Not wind; closer, like a pulse buried in the soil. The sound tugged at something familiar deep in her chest.

Julie looked over her shoulder. The trees looked the same, but their shadows had changed angle.

"You're fine," she whispered. Her voice disappeared into the damp.

She followed the creek upstream, counting steps. At thirty-seven she stopped. Across the water, a shape interrupted the pattern of trunks: tall, coat dark, hat brim low. He stood as if he had always been there.

Her throat went dry.

"Hello?" she called, because silence felt worse.

The man didn't move. A watch chain caught a thread of light and winked once. Then he was gone—no retreating rustle, no displaced branch, only absence.

Julie forced a thin laugh. "You're seeing things, genius."

But the forest had gone still. Even her pulse felt borrowed. She crouched by the water again. Its surface trembled, forming shapes she couldn't name—letters maybe, or the thought of them. A ripple reached her boot, though nothing had fallen in.

She looked down. Her reflection was pale, distorted, mouth open. Behind it, another mouth formed the same word a heartbeat late.

Her breath caught. The undertone beneath her feet deepened, rising through bone.

The world tilted. Pain lanced her skull; the ground rushed up. Somewhere in the fall she heard her own voice from far away: He said he loved me. Then he cut me open like a rag doll. Where's Pearl?

Water flashed. Stones hammered her hip. Then—black.

A hand shook her shoulder. Her father's breath—coffee and wintergreen. "Julie! Honey, wake up."

Her eyes fluttered open to the blur of needles overhead. "Dad?"

He exhaled hard. "You fainted."

She turned her head. Beyond him, a figure stood by the tree line—hat brim low, moustache a shadow. He watched them the way people watch clocks.

"Do you see him?" she whispered.

Frank glanced back. The bank was empty.

"I came because you screamed," he said gently. "What happened?"

"I don't know. He was there and then he wasn't. He called me—" She swallowed. "He called me Julie."

Frank's eyes flicked over her face, cataloging color, pupils, breath. "We're going inside."

Her mother was already at the sink, sleeves rolled, hands wet. "What happened? Is she dizzy? Did you hydrate? Julie—look at me."

"I'm not sick," Julie said, though her tongue felt wrong in her mouth.

Leslie moved like she did in the lab—fast, precise. Thermometer, pulse, color. "Vitals fine. Possibly low blood sugar."

"She saw someone in the woods," Frank said quietly.

Leslie stilled. "A camper?"

Julie shook her head. "He said my name, but... not my name."

Leslie searched her daughter's face for rational entry points. "Maybe you dreamed. Hypoxia from fainting."

"Mom, I wasn't dreaming."

Frank rubbed Julie's back. "It's okay. Let's sit, yeah?"

But the quiet after his words made the kitchen smaller. The refrigerator's note flattened into a single tone—too steady, almost like breathing.

Leslie forced a smile. "We'll test a theory. Light refraction can make you see things that aren't there." She grabbed the handheld mirror from the counter, angled it toward the window. "See? Just angles."

Julie looked. For a second, the glass showed only them—the family triangle of worry and love. Then her reflection blinked out of rhythm with her body.

Her mother's smile faltered. "It's glare."

Frank stepped closer. "Leslie—"

The light steadied. The reflection matched again. Leslie exhaled. "See? Glare."

But Julie had already stepped back. The smell in the room changed—less kitchen, more hospital, that faint metallic sweetness that doesn't belong to food. Beneath it, a soft hiss, like air escaping a pipe.

"I need air," Julie whispered, and before they could stop her, she pushed out the screen door.

Night fell fast in the trees. It always did here—one moment day, next moment the forest wrapped its own echo around the cabin. Her mother made soup that grew cold in bowls. Her father tuned the radio to a station that hummed more than it sang. When Julie closed her eyes, the dark behind them rippled like water.

She dreamed in pieces: a room tiled white; a man with careful hands and a smile that had learned patience. A woman's voice that sounded like hers and didn't: Don't open your eyes.

When her own voice woke her, she was already sitting up. Her mother's silhouette bent over her. Her father's shadow filled the doorway.

"What did I say?"

"You called a name," her father answered after a beat. "Julie."

"That's not me."

"I know."

They waited for morning the way sailors wait for wind—together, but in silence.

At breakfast, the pancakes went uneaten. Leslie's hands shook when she poured coffee; Frank pretended not to notice. The decision not to speak had its own gravity.

Julie stepped onto the porch to test the air. It tasted like rain that had forgotten to fall.

At the tree line she stopped. The man stood between two pines, as far away as before, as still. She tried to lift a hand, but her body went quiet. Her mouth opened.

"Before death claims my soul," she whispered, voice not her own, "I curse you to wander in purgatory. Your torment shall be my redemption."

The screen door banged like a gunshot. Her father's arms were around her a second later, a circle warm enough to argue with the cold moving under her skin.

"Jules. Breathe."

She did. He breathed with her. The man between the pines tilted his head, curious, then folded back into the trunks the way shadows do when clouds take the sun.

Her mother stood in the doorway, white to the mouth. "We're leaving," she said, voice made of glass. "After breakfast. Or before."

Frank nodded slowly. "After. We'll stop at Harold's."

Inside, the mirror over the sink showed only the room. That should have felt like mercy. It didn't.

The antiseptic scent lingered, then thinned.

Julie found her notebook and drew the man's watch chain in three strokes—curve, glint, weight. She pressed the page until the paper took the mark twice.

She didn't write a name. She didn't have to.

Outside, the forest pretended it had only ever been trees. Inside, the pancakes cooled, ordinary and untouched. And somewhere between them, the house waited to see who would look first.

2

THE CABIN

The highway unspooled in ribbons of mist and memory. Headlights smeared across fog, every mile marker flashing like a pulse she couldn't match. Julie's hands tightened on the wheel. The wipers kept a slow, hypnotic rhythm, clearing the windshield only for the world to blur again.

Chicago had vanished hours ago, but its noise still echoed inside her, the city undertone that refused to die even when silence begged for room. Somewhere between gas stations and cornfields, she'd started talking to herself, testing her own voice against the hush.

"You're fine," she said aloud, though her ghost in the side window said nothing back.

The dashboard clock flickered: 4:17 A.M. She'd been driving since midnight, chasing the direction her nightmares pointed. The radio died an hour in, replaced by a faint sibilance that rose and fell. Twice she reached to switch it off, and twice she didn't, listening for a pattern, half expecting it to say her name.

Fog thickened until the road ended a few feet ahead. Her high beams caught the suggestion of trees, wet bark glinting like muscle under skin. For a heartbeat, the light carved a shape—tall, dark, still—then it vanished, swallowed. Julie's pulse kicked hard against her ribs.

"Not again," she whispered, gripping the wheel tighter. "Not tonight."

She rolled the window down; air smelling of rain and asphalt pushed through, grounding her. Ahead, the first pale seam of dawn bled across the horizon. Somewhere beyond it waited her parents' house, coffee, the illusion of safety.

The road unwound through gray fields. The wipers kept time. She tried to focus on the ordinary—mile markers, the road's low thrum—but the city followed in afterimages: a corridor lit too white, a patient whispering, Julia, before his monitor went flat.

At the time she'd blamed exhaustion, neurons cross-wiring grief into déjà vu. But now, alone in the fog, she couldn't stop hearing that word, as if the man hadn't spoken to her at all but through her.

She drove faster, chasing distance she couldn't define. The lines on the asphalt blurred into one thread pulling her north.

The fog lifted with the dawn, revealing suburbs softened by gray. Streetlights clicked off one by one. When she turned into her parents' drive, her headlights brushed the porch steps and found her father waiting, two mugs steaming beside him. For a moment, pressure broke in her chest.

Frank lifted a hand. His silhouette was steady, the outline of the one constant she trusted.

"You're up early," she said, killing the engine. Her voice came rough from hours of silence.

He smiled, creases brightening in the half-light. "Your mother told me you were heading to the woods. You didn't think I'd let you go alone, did you?"

Relief struck sharp and sudden. She stepped into his arms, the warmth of coffee and shaving soap familiar as prayer. The mugs knocked, splashing dark liquid onto the porch boards.

"I haven't slept," she murmured. "The dreams came back. The man—he's the same. I don't know what's happening to me."

Frank held her tighter, breathing even, the rhythm he'd taught her years ago for calming storms. "Then we'll face it together, peanut. You drive yourself too hard. Let me take the wheel this time."

A brittle laugh slipped out, half sob and half surrender. "Deal."

They stood until the chill bit. He passed her a mug and gestured toward the sunrise. "Drink before it cools. Coffee fixes most things. Not all, but most."

The porch smelled of cedar and wet earth. Somewhere in the trees, a bird tested its voice and fell silent again.

Inside, the house felt smaller than memory. Her mother's plants crowded every sill—green lungs drinking what little light the fog allowed. Photographs lined the mantle: birthdays, graduations, the old camping trip where she stood between her parents, gap-toothed grin and wild hair, a butterfly net almost bigger than she was. She'd sworn she'd catch something blue.

Her mother had laughed. *We don't trap miracles, we just notice them.*

The memory stung like someone else's dream.

"I packed light," Julie said, glancing at the duffel. "Didn't want to spook Mom."

"She knows," Frank said softly. "Maybe not all the details. But she always knows."

Julie nodded, grateful for his restraint. "Then let's go before I change my mind."

He chuckled, that low sound from thunderstorms. "You and me both."

They loaded the truck in silence—the easy kind, built from years of shared work. Zippers, trunk, footsteps. The grammar of family.

The highway north unspooled under a pewter sky. Clouds pressed low, smudging treetops. Julie drifted between wakefulness and memory: her father's steady hand, the soft murmur of classic rock, the scent of coffee.

By afternoon, the forest deepened around them. The hum of the tires steadied her until something under it began to pulse—a faint vibration, like a second meter in the chassis. She opened her mouth to mention it, then stopped. Frank's jaw was tight, his knuckles white. He heard it too. He just chose not to name it.

"You all right, Jules?" he asked after a minute, voice light, too casual.

"I'm fine." The word was automatic, wrong in her mouth.

He reached across the console, hand finding hers. "We'll stock up, get some rest. You'll feel better with a routine again."

Routine. Normal. Words like furniture in a house already burning. Julie nodded anyway.

Outside, the trees shifted. For a moment, they seemed to bend inward, as if the forest itself were listening.

The town appeared out of fog—one stoplight, one diner, a grocery with a green awning dulled by rain. Frank parked out front. "Grab what we need and hit the road," he said. "If Harold's still there, we can say hi."

The bell over the door chimed flatly. Lights buzzed overhead, flickering between shades of white too bright to be comfortable. The air smelled of lemon cleaner and dust. Julie's shoes squeaked on linoleum—each step echoing back a half-beat late, as if the room were learning her.

"Canned peaches or pears?" Frank called from an aisle over.

"Doesn't matter," she said, voice hollow. She stared at the rows until the letters blurred into loops. The fluorescents thinned into something too regular to be random. A whisper threaded through it.

Julia.

Her breath hitched. She turned sharply. At the aisle's far end, a man stood—hands clasped behind his back, hat brim low, a watch chain winking once. He watched her with the calm of someone certain of the outcome.

Then he was gone.

"Julie?"

Her father's voice shattered the stillness. She blinked, heart pounding. Her cart was half full—groceries she didn't remember choosing. Frank rounded the corner, reading her face like an emergency.

"You're white as paper," he said. "Sit down before you fall."

"I—he was here," she managed. "The man from the woods."

He swallowed hard but kept his tone steady. "You saw someone who reminded you of him. That's all."

Before she could argue, another voice boomed behind them.

"Well, I'll be damned! Frank Simmons—twenty years and not a day older!"

Relief flashed across Frank's face. "Harold Gentshaft," he said, laughing. "Wasn't sure you still owned this place."

They clasped hands. For a heartbeat, normalcy tried to return. But when Harold looked at Julie, his grin faltered. "That can't be little Julie."

"All grown up," Frank said. "Vet in Chicago now."

She tried to mirror the smile, but the tubes overhead flickered twice, then stuttered out of sync. In the freezer door beside Harold, the shine didn't reflect him at all. It held a brimmed hat, a faint moustache, a chain catching false light.

Julie's breath hitched. "Dad," she whispered. "Can we go?"

He followed her gaze, saw only his own face, and nodded. "Sure."

The drive back passed in silence. The sky darkened to bruised violet. Raindrops struck the windshield—soft, deliberate. Each sounded less like water and more like footsteps on tile. Julie tried to count them, but the rhythm kept changing.

Frank cleared his throat. "You okay back there?"

She nodded, though her reflection in the glass shook its head. "I'm fine."

He gave the same small smile he'd used when she was little and scared of nothing visible. "We'll call your mom once we unload. She'll want proof we survived Harold's coffee."

The attempt at levity loosened something in her chest. She almost laughed, then didn't. The air between them felt charged, as if the truck itself were exhaling.

Fog thickened until the road turned to gravel. The forest rose to meet them, branches bent inward like hands against glass. When the headlights cut through, she thought she saw movement between the trunks—something walking parallel, matching speed, just beyond the beam.

"Dad."

"Hmm?"

"Do you see—"

When she looked again, there was only fog.

The cabin appeared through the mist, windows dull with condensation, roofline sagging like a breath held too long. Frank parked near the porch and killed the engine. "Home sweet haunted home," he said lightly, but his eyes lingered on the trees a beat too long.

Julie managed a laugh that didn't reach her throat. She gathered the bags, following him up the steps. The porch boards groaned.

Inside, the air changed—denser, alert. Her skin prickled. The scent of rain had been replaced by something colder, metallic, a faint tang like ozone before lightning.

"Smells like a storm," Frank said, though the rain had stopped.

Julie tried to answer, but dizziness hit. The bags slipped; cans rolled in dull percussion.

"Julie?"

Her vision fractured—light bending, air thickening. The undertone returned, low at first, then rising until it filled her teeth. It moved through her, matching her heart.

A whisper rode beneath, soft and certain.

You will always be mine, Julia.

Her knees buckled. Frank caught her, groceries forgotten. Her head lolled against his shoulder, breath shallow, skin cold as tile.

"Julie, talk to me," he said, shaking her gently.

Her lips moved once, a whisper escaping that wasn't hers. "Julia."

Frank eased her onto the couch, fingers trembling at her pulse. For a terrible moment he couldn't find it. Then—faint, fluttering. He exhaled a prayer she didn't hear.

Outside, the rain stopped altogether. The silence that followed felt alive, thick with waiting.

Frank brushed her hair back. "You're okay," he whispered, his voice breaking on the lie. The overhead light flickered once, twice, then steadied. The air smelled faintly of burnt wires.

Three beats. Slow. Deliberate.

He turned toward the window, careful not to move the curtain. The glass fogged with his breath, then cleared. The forest stood still, listening.

At first he thought the noise was blood in his ears. Then he realized it came from the walls—a vibration, rhythmic, almost human.

Julie's voice came small and clear. "Do you hear that?"

He nodded. "Yeah. I hear it."

Neither spoke the truth.

The thrum faded, leaving only a trace of ozone and iron.

"Old pipes," Frank said. "We'll check it tomorrow."

Julie didn't answer. Her gaze had fixed on the ceiling, where the plaster trembled ever so slightly, as if the house itself were breathing.

Outside, fog pressed against the windows.

The cabin listened.

And in its listening, something woke.

3

THE SLOW GRIP

Frank drove with both hands locked at ten and two, knuckles pale. Wipers dragged through thin rain. Beside him, Julie watched trees blur past, her reflection faint in the window—eyes distant, mouth drawn. He tried not to look too long, afraid he'd see that other shadow slide over her face again.

The town still fit a single intersection: post office, diner, Harold's grocery. The kind of place that pretended time had been merciful. Frank's chest tightened. Some ghosts didn't need faces; they wore places.

Inside, the bell over the door gave its tired jangle. The lights buzzed their sterile tune, and for a heartbeat, it almost felt ordinary.

Julie drifted the aisles like someone underwater. Frank kept half an eye on her as he collected the essentials—eggs, bread, coffee, anything that made him feel capable. He turned, and there she was again at the freezer case, breath fogging the glass as if she peered through to another time.

"Jules?" he said gently.

She blinked, startled. Her hands trembled, as if only now remembering how to belong to her body. "I'm fine."

"You're not," he said softly, as if admitting it too loudly would summon what he feared.

"Frank Simmons!" boomed a familiar voice. "As I live and breathe."

Frank exhaled a grateful smile. "Harold." They shook hands like men who once believed the world stayed predictable if you stayed busy. "Still running this place?"

"Someone's got to keep the lights humming," Harold said, grinning. Then his gaze slid to Julie. "Well, I'll be damned. Little Julie Simmons, all grown up."

Julie offered a polite nod. The overhead tubes flickered. For an instant, the freezer's chrome edge held a different outline—black suit, a wink of watch chain. The grin behind the glass turned sharper. Julie's breath caught; she stepped back into the cart.

"Dad," she whispered. "Can we go?"

Frank saw her face and didn't question it. "Harold, I'll catch up tonight. I owe you a beer."

"You owe me a few," Harold said, eyes following Julie with quiet unease.

Rain followed them home in fine mist. The road wound upward, trees closing around it like ribs. Frank kept watching the woods, half expecting movement. The forest felt different—crowded, aware. As if it had learned their names.

When the cabin came into view, windows fogged, he felt a pull in his chest—grief mixed with recognition. Leslie had loved this place. She'd called it "controlled wilderness," a lab for wonder. Now the house looked like a body remembering breath.

THE DEVIL INSIDE

Inside, the air was cooler than it should have been. He set the bags on the counter, turned to Julie. "Breathe with me," he said quietly. "In. Out."

The old trick. It had calmed her during storms, steadied her after nightmares. She obeyed—then the air shifted, subtle but unmistakable. The undertone under the floorboards deepened. Julie's gaze unfocused, sliding past him to the window.

"Julie?"

Her pupils dilated, swallowing the green. Temperature dropped so fast his breath turned visible.

"Julie," he repeated, stepping closer.

Her lips parted, but the voice wasn't hers. "You ran once," it murmured, low and cold. "You won't run again."

Frank's training was grief, not medicine, but his hands moved anyway—checking pulse, grounding her wrists, counting aloud to tether himself to time. "Stay with me, peanut." His voice shook.

Her eyes rolled white, then darkened—ink spilling through until color was gone. The smile that curved her mouth was wrong, too composed. "Julia," the voice said. "Mine."

"Stop." He didn't know who he addressed—his daughter or the thing inside. "Who are you?"

The answer came like breath on glass. "Closer than breath. Older than your science."

Her back arched. The sound that tore from her throat wasn't human—it was a body remembering pain. Frank pressed a palm to her forehead. Cold. Reason slid away like oil—seizure, psychosis, oxygen deprivation—labels with no grip.

"Frank?" a voice called from outside.

He jolted. "Harold?" He looked down—Julie's breathing had steadied. Her eyes fluttered open, color returning like dawn. She looked at him with confused exhaustion.

"Stay here," he said, though every cell screamed not to leave her.

He opened the door to rain and pine. Harold stood on the porch, a case of beer tucked under one arm. "Brought the good kind," he said, eyes narrowing. "You all right? You look like you saw a ghost."

"Something like that. Come in."

Behind him, Julie whispered, almost inaudible. "I hear him."

The walls seemed to lean closer.

Harold didn't stay long—polite sentences, shared silence, a promise to visit tomorrow. When he left, the air felt heavier, as if something unseen had followed him to the tree line and stopped.

Frank locked the door. The sound cracked like a shot.

Julie was asleep—or pretending. Her fingers twitched, curling like someone reaching for an invisible hand. He sat beside her, listening to shallow breaths. He'd done this once before—with Leslie, when machines breathed for her. Back then he'd promised to protect what was left.

He found Julie's old steno pad on the side table and began to write.

Subject J.S.—episode two. Duration unknown. Auditory and visual dissociation; self-reference loss. Secondary voice male, late 19th c. syntax. Environmental shift: temperature drop $\approx 10°F$. Working thought—psychogenic; contagious delusion possible.

He stared at the words—safety nets woven from disbelief. Every letter trembled. Leslie would have known what to do. *If I can measure it, I can control it*, she'd said once. Science as prayer.

"Leslie," he whispered. "Tell me what to do."

The silence wasn't empty. It listened.

The rain eased. He rose and went to the sink. The faucet dripped once, twice. Each drop landed with a clock's precision. Beneath it, another rhythm—steady, deliberate.

It's in the walls. Or under them.

A draft slipped through—cold as exhaled breath. The resonance deepened until he felt it in his teeth. He turned toward the hallway.

Light leaked from under Julie's door—flickering, sterile. The smell of phenol reached him first, sharp and chemical, a ghost from the past. His stomach clenched.

He stepped closer. The mirror on the far wall reflected his movement, but the image answered late.

"Julie?" he called.

Her voice floated from inside, thin, layered. "He's back."

Frank's reflection stared back, but the eyes were wrong—dark pits for pupils, expression too calm. Light behind the glass thickened, resolving into motion: a tiled room, a figure leaning over a table.

He whispered before he could stop himself. "Julia."

The woman in the reflection turned. Her face was Julie's and not Julie's—older, colder, eyes filled with the sadness of someone who'd already died. She lifted a gloved hand and pressed it to the other side of the glass.

Condensation parted beneath her touch. Frost veined outward, webbing the mirror. Temperature plunged. His breath fogged, merging with hers across the glass.

Frank's hand rose on instinct. The instant his fingers met the frost, cold burned through him, crawling up his arm like quicksilver. Soap and iron. Beneath it—the hiss of gas.

The reflection moved with eerie precision. Behind the woman, shadows converged: Holmes's shape, blurred but smiling.

Julie stirred behind him. "He's writing again," she whispered, voice slurred by exhaustion. "Through me."

Frank spun. Her eyes were open but unfocused. He pulled her from the mirror's glow. Frost cracked with the sound of strained glass. The undertone spiked to one note, then cut off.

Julie sagged against him, trembling. "He's not done," she said.

He held her tighter. "Neither am I."

By dawn she slept, skin pale but peaceful. Frank sat at the kitchen table, the steno pad before him. The page from last night stared back—tidy handwriting marching toward the impossible. He turned to a fresh sheet.

Environmental response noted. Structure demonstrates sentience correlated with occupant distress. Working thought: House functions as resonant conduit, not origin.

He underlined not origin twice. His pulse jumped as he noticed the second line slant upward, letters sharper, older, as if written by someone else.

He blinked. The ink looked fresh. A bead trembled, spreading like it was alive.

He looked up. The light flickered once, steadied. Then the sound began—not electric, but mechanical. Slow. Deliberate. Rhythmic.

A typewriter.

Keys struck somewhere below—metal to metal. One keystroke at a time. Between each: the whisper of pages turning.

He rose. The basement door was shut, but the handle quivered softly, keeping time.

The air tasted of carbon and dust.

He stepped closer, heart pounding until it joined the rhythm. The typing paused, as if it, too, were listening. Then it resumed—two words, deliberate, each letter a verdict.

He pressed his ear to the door.

Continuity maintained.

The handle stilled. Silence followed—thick, final.

Frank backed away, afraid to disturb the quiet. The undertone returned to the walls, lower now, satisfied.

He sat again and picked up the pen with shaking fingers. On the next blank line, in handwriting that wasn't quite his, words appeared as if written from under the page.

We remember what you forget.

He dropped the pen. The house sighed—boards settling—but the sound felt too measured to be random.

Upstairs, Julie stirred. A soft murmur: "Pearl."

Frank pressed his palms to the table until his knuckles went white. The wood was warm—too warm.

He killed the light and sat in the dark, listening to the drip in the pipes, the faint vibration under his feet.

When dawn crept through the window, it caught the edge of the steno pad. The ink shimmered gold before dulling to black.

The cabin exhaled. Somewhere deep beneath the floorboards, the typewriter answered with a single key—struck once like a heartbeat.

4

The First Night

Night came without ceremony, sliding over the pines like a second skin. The storm had passed, leaving the air washed and listening. The cabin seemed to relax, wood and glass easing into quiet.

Frank sat at the table with his notebook open, the lamp turned low enough that its light was unsteady. The page waited for reason—clean, ruled, expectant. He'd always trusted paper; it had boundaries. Paper couldn't lie. Tonight the lines blurred, his handwriting crawling like it didn't want to be known.

00:04 — Subject J.S. Resting. Vitals steady. Environmental undertone ≈ 65 Hz. Source: unknown.

He stopped, pencil hovering. Graphite left a gray bruise on the margin. The sound wasn't mechanical; it changed when he breathed.

He rubbed at the ache behind his eye. Leslie would've called it another migraine. He could almost hear her: Hydrate. Step away from the page. But she would've known he wouldn't. Her memory felt close tonight, not nostalgia but pressure—a weight behind his ribs. He pictured her fingers, fine-boned and confident, stained from lab work. If Leslie were here, he thought, she'd tell me to stop measuring the dead.

The lamp flickered. The air shifted—sweet, sharp, antiseptic. Ether, or something pretending to be it. The smell knifed through memory. White tile. A whisper at his ear. He blinked until the present returned, then forced his hand to move.

00:17 — Odor detected (ether/phenol). Duration 7s. No visible source.

The table vibrated beneath his wrist, faint but metered. He flattened his palm. The tremor matched his pulse.

"Sound is vibration," he murmured. "Vibration needs air." Saying it steadied him like a prayer.

The tone changed—one long rise, almost curious.

He froze. "Acknowledgment," he whispered, absurdly, and still the word fit.

A thin line of light leaked from beneath Julie's door upstairs. He hadn't left her lamp on. The hair along his arms rose.

He stood, taking the notebook. Logic might not save him, but it could keep him company.

Halfway up the steps, the temperature fell. Ether deepened, touched now with rust. The undertone vibrated through the railing into his bones. Two pulses. Pause. Two more. The rhythm of breathing.

"Julie?"

No answer. The light under the door widened, colorless and bright. Too sterile for a home.

He pushed the door.

The room glowed like a submerged world. Julie lay still, lips shaping words that made no sound. The mirror opposite her bed repeated the motion a half-beat late—learning her.

He crossed the floor. "Hey. Jules."

Her eyes opened. Not green. Not black. Absence—holes punched through reality.

The bulb overhead flared white, humming once before bursting. Shards scattered across the quilt. The undertone collapsed, replaced by a silence so absolute his heartbeat popped inside his skull.

"Julie." He caught her wrist. Pulse fluttering—wild, alive.

Her mouth opened again. Two voices came out.

"You always run," it said first.

A pause, then colder: "You left her on the table."

Precise. Surgical. Not accusation—documentation.

Frank turned to the mirror. His reflection watched him, but something leaned behind it: a man in a dark coat, indistinct face, a watch chain swaying to the room's meter.

He stepped in front of Julie. "Who are you?"

The reflection smiled. Frost spread from the mirror's center, veining outward like skin. Each breath made the ice bloom; each exhale cleared it—revealing flashes of tile, a basin swirling red, the bright hiss of gas.

Phenol burned the air.

Julie sat upright. Her voice was a whisper carved from someone else's throat. "She's not done."

"Don't look," he said. "Don't."

The mirror convulsed. A single crack split the surface—a lightning bolt through water. Cold rolled out, hugging the floor, creeping up his legs.

A voice followed, smooth, pleased: "Continuity maintained."

He grabbed the blanket from the bed and threw it over the mirror. The glass exhaled—a sigh that came from everywhere at once.

Then silence.

He held Julie until the tremor left her limbs. "It's all right," he lied. "It's over."

"She said my name," Julie murmured. "Not Julie. Julia."

He looked toward the covered glass. "Dreams echo. They use whatever's near."

She shook her head. "Then why does it know what she looks like?"

He couldn't answer. The air warmed; ether thinned to dust. Beneath the floorboards, something tapped—slow, deliberate, like a pulse rehearsing.

He sat on the edge of her bed, notebook across his knees.

01:54 — Auditory/visual phenomena shared.
Temp drop $\approx$ 15°F. No electrical cause observed.

He hesitated, then wrote the sentence that broke his faith:

She spoke through our daughter.

The pencil snapped. He didn't notice until graphite smeared his knuckles.

Julie drifted into uneasy sleep. Her lips still moved, whispering to someone unseen. The blanket over the mirror sagged, too heavy for cloth.

Data, he told himself. Collect data.

He counted her breaths, syncing his own until calm felt possible. For a moment, fragile peace. Then the undertone returned—slow, patient—as if thought itself had learned rhythm.

He thought of Leslie again—her laugh when he muttered field notes, her hand on his back until the world righted. "Leslie," he whispered now. Not summoning. Anchoring.

Her name steadied him long enough to stand.

Dawn peeled night away by degrees. The undertone receded like tide, leaving quiet. When he turned the lamp on, it behaved. He pulled the blanket down.

The mirror was whole. Condensation gathered near its base, letters forming in slow motion.

I remain.

He touched them. The glass was warm—heartbeat-warm.

Downstairs, the kettle began to whistle though the stove was cold. The sound wasn't shrill—it was steady, human, breath filtered through metal. A ring of moisture marked the counter, perfect as an incision circle.

Julie's footsteps came behind him. "Morning?"

He turned. She looked younger and farther away, drained of color. She clutched her mother's scarf, twisting it between her fingers.

"Morning," he said. "Coffee's on."

"I dreamed about a room," she said. "No windows. Light that never turned off."

"We'll go into town," he said, forcing calm. "Sarah's diner—pie, sunlight, normal things."

"She's still here," Julie whispered. "Watching from the glass."

"Then we won't look at glass."

Outside, fog threaded the pines, turning sunlight silver. Birds shook rain from their wings, the world rehearsing normal.

Inside, the air vibrated faintly—an overtone both of them pretended not to hear.

"Finish packing," Frank said. "We'll leave soon."

Julie nodded, winding the scarf tighter around her wrist as if it could keep her tethered. When she passed the window, her reflection lagged a heartbeat behind, then caught up.

He waited until she was gone to open the notebook.

06:42 — Phenomenon persists at lower amplitude. Correlation between heartbeat and resonance confirmed.

He hesitated, pencil trembling.

Continuity—

The pencil began to tap, soft, deliberate. A steady rhythm against the page.

He froze. It wasn't his hand.

The sound deepened until it became a pulse he could feel.

He looked up. The windowpane quivered. In its reflection, the blanket over the mirror upstairs was moving—rising, falling, like breath.

He closed the notebook and let it tap, his heart syncing to its rhythm.

Outside, morning brightened. Inside, the undertone matched daylight's expansion—measured, patient, alive.

The house seemed to inhale.

And somewhere between breath and hush, the voice returned—faint but certain.

"Continuity maintained."

5
Harold's Ledger

The grocery store had gone still hours ago. The freezers breathed in their sleep, and the air smelled of wet cardboard, coffee, and lemon polish. Harold Gentshaft sat behind the counter, the stool creaking in time with the rain against the windows. The storm hadn't decided to leave—it lingered like memory, heavy and unfinished.

He should have locked up. One more cup of coffee, he kept telling himself. Then another. The mug beside him had cooled twice.

The ledger lay open like a wound—brown leather, edges soft as cloth, its title burned into the cover: City Records, 1889.

It had come from a box of donations the historical society sent two weeks earlier. Most of it had been dull—receipts, ration lists, birth records—but this one wasn't.

The paper felt rough, as if it had once been soaked and dried too quickly. The ink was still black after a century, refusing to fade. Every page began the same way: Experiment, Observation, Result.

Harold traced the latest entry he'd dared to read:

Experiment 12 – Subject Simmons, J.
Result: Deferred.

He frowned. "Deferred to what?"

The ceiling fan clicked overhead, off-beat, like a metronome remembering a song. Rain on the glass sounded like someone taking notes in Morse code.

He leaned closer. The handwriting was mechanical—sharp, deliberate. He'd seen it before. He'd built a career on recognizing it.

Holmes's hand.

He'd lectured on it at the historical society—The Murder Castle Diaries: Madness and Modernity. He used to joke that Holmes's real immortality wasn't his crimes but his documentation. The doctor hadn't murdered for pleasure or money. He'd done it for continuity.

He'd meant it as metaphor then. Tonight, it didn't feel like one.

He turned the page. The lines slanted tighter, the pen pressing deeper into the paper.

Continuity test successful. Site relocated beneath municipal property. Monitoring continues.

He mouthed the words. The undertone from the coolers deepened until it thrummed through his ribs.

"Monitoring continues," he repeated. The phrase rang wrong.

A chill crawled up his neck. 12:07 a.m. Frank Simmons would be up at the cabin by now, trying to fix whatever haunted that family.

Harold had known Frank for years—hunted deer with him, shared more burnt coffee than their wives approved of. Frank was steady, pragmatic. For him to call last week, voice shaking, leaving that message—If anything happens, check the ledger—had frozen something deep inside Harold's chest.

He reached for the phone. No dial tone. Only a low hiss, steady as breath.

"Lines are wet," he muttered. "That's all."

He didn't believe it.

The storm pressed harder against the glass. For a second, the reflection in the window lagged—his movements delayed half a beat. The man behind the counter blinked slower.

Harold's hand tightened around the mug. "Jesus," he whispered.

The reflection smiled.

Then it was gone. The lights flickered, steadied.

He turned back to the ledger. The words had changed. The ink bled into fresh lines:

Harold Gentshaft — Addendum: Monitoring Resumed.

He stared until the letters darkened. "Frank," he breathed, "what did you drag me into?"

The ceiling fan stopped. The freezers went silent. The only sound was the rain ticking against glass.

He tried to close the book. It resisted, vibrating faintly beneath his palms. Pages turned themselves—whss, whss—as if someone flipped them from within.

Subject H.H.H.—continuity assured.

The vibration climbed through his teeth. The windows fogged from the inside, shaping words in condensation:

He Remembers.

Harold lurched to his feet, stool clattering. The sound didn't echo; it was swallowed whole.

He grabbed his jacket and shoved the ledger inside. The leather burned cold against his chest. "Not staying," he muttered. "Not part of this."

The bell over the door jangled as he pushed through, but the chime dragged behind him—a beat too late.

Outside, rain struck his face like applause. The street was empty except for the reflections. They moved slower than he did, mouths shaping words he couldn't hear.

He hurried across the parking lot to his truck. The air smelled faintly of phenol and dust—the scent of a place cleaned for an autopsy.

He slid inside, slammed the door, jammed the key into the ignition.

The radio came on by itself—static threaded with a heartbeat.

Sequence maintained.

He twisted the dial off. The vibration didn't stop. It lived in the steering wheel, in the metal, in him.

He drove.

Main Street blurred past in streaks of gray and gold. Rain washed the world to water and reflection. The town dissolved behind him—except for the faint glow of the historical society window, still lit.

He hesitated, then pulled over.

Inside, the air was stale with lemon cleaner and old photographs. Rows of display cases reflected the flicker of fluorescent bulbs. He had curated half this museum himself—Holmes's letters, floor plans of the Murder Castle, rusted tools displayed like relics.

He walked the aisle slowly, boots squeaking.

The undertone followed.

At the back, one case glowed faintly. Condensation clouded the inside of the glass. Words formed through the fog in elegant handwriting:

You always believed, Harold. That's why you were chosen.

He backed away. "No," he whispered. "I just study."

Study becomes faith.

The glass cracked from the inside, a single surgical line. The floor shifted beneath him.

From the archive room came a soft rustling, like paper turning itself.

He swallowed. "Frank, what the hell did you find?"

The archive door stood open, light spilling across the hall. The air shimmered, like heat over asphalt.

He stepped inside.

Every folder had opened. Pages hovered an inch above their boxes, turning slowly, whispering like restless wings. His own handwriting glowed among the older script—lecture notes, research annotations—but beneath them, someone had written new words in that same slanted Victorian hand:

Continuity: transferred to observer.

Witness becomes subject.

The ledger in his jacket pulsed again. He pulled it free. The ink on its open page was still wet.

Observation transferred.

Subject: F. Simmons.

And beneath it, still forming:

Witness Gentshaft — Secondary Custodian.

The words burned cold against his chest.

"Frank," he said aloud, "you've got no idea what this thing really is."

At last he understood—the ledger wasn't a diary. It was a mechanism. Holmes hadn't recorded his killings to remember them. He'd recorded them to persist.

Every experiment created an observer. Every observer became an experiment.

The vibration deepened until the light fixtures trembled.

From the corner, one framed photograph slid off the wall and hit the tile face-up. Glass shattered.

He looked down. The picture had changed.

It showed the inside of the grocery store—his counter, his stool, the ledger open. Behind the counter sat Harold himself, pen in hand.

The image shimmered once, then reverted to Holmes's portrait.

Harold's knees nearly gave. He grabbed the ledger, clutching it like a weapon. The pages fluttered again:

Continue the monitoring.

"No," he said through his teeth. "I'm ending it."

He stuffed the ledger into his coat and turned toward the exit. For a moment, everything went still. Even the vibration stopped.

Then came silence so perfect it hurt.

A second passed. Another.

Then the entire building exhaled—air through vents, the pop of old wood—as if the place itself had been holding its breath.

The photographs on the walls all turned at once, facing him.

He ran.

The bell over the front door screamed when he yanked it open, the sound splitting the night. Rain poured in, silver under the streetlight.

He stumbled into the street, the storm wrapping him in cold applause.

Lightning flashed. For an instant, a figure stood in the center of Main Street—dark coat, hat brim low, hands clasped behind his back.

Holmes.

"Stay dead," Harold whispered, voice breaking.

He threw himself into the truck, slammed the door, and started the engine.

The ledger on the seat beside him snapped open. Pages fluttered, ink spilling itself across the paper faster than he could breathe.

Experiment 27 — Observer Harold Gentshaft.
Result: Pending.

He gripped the wheel until his knuckles burned. "Not this time," he said. "I decide the result."

He pulled the replica Holmes quill from his pocket and scrawled across the page with shaking hands:

Result: Resistance. Monitoring interrupted.

The vibration changed pitch. The truck's lights dimmed, then brightened. Rain fell harder, each drop striking the windshield in perfect rhythm with the pulse.

Lightning struck close, painting the interior gold. The ink shimmered before turning black.

He exhaled, unsteady, and looked up.

Across the fogged windshield, new words formed in reverse, written from the outside:

Resistance acknowledged.
Sequence altered.

The vibration softened—less threat now, more curiosity.

Harold leaned back against the seat. "Yeah," he whispered. "Let's see you write that in."

He drove.

The ledger stayed quiet. The hum receded to a faint thrum under his ribs—the ghost of a heartbeat.

Main Street dissolved behind him, streetlights flickering one by one like punctuation.

He didn't know where Frank and Julie were, or how deep they'd fallen, but he finally understood what the book wanted.

It didn't crave blood. It craved witnesses.

And tonight, it had lost one.

He reached for the radio.

Static answered—soft, slow, threaded with the faint sound of pages turning.

He smiled grimly. "Keep reading," he said. "I'm done writing."

Outside, the storm eased, rain thinning to mist.

Far ahead, the road bent toward the woods. The ledger warmed against his side, pulsing faintly, leading him north.

Harold didn't fight it.

Not yet.

6

Harold's Pursuit

Harold Gentshaft hadn't planned to chase ghosts after retirement.

He'd planned on crossword puzzles, cheap whiskey, and ignoring the whispers in Chicago's concrete whenever another construction crew unearthed a relic that didn't belong to this century. But the city had other plans. Holmes always did.

It began with a headline: POST OFFICE RENOVATION HALTED AFTER UNEXPLAINED STRUCTURAL COLLAPSE.

The story ran for two days before politics buried it, but Harold saved the clipping anyway. He recognized the address. Section C—the same ground his great-grandfather had helped build. The same one his family had been paid handsomely never to discuss.

He told himself it was curiosity when he packed his tool bag again. Not guilt.

By the time he reached the south edge of the city, rain had begun—thin and patient, the kind that blurred everything except regret.

The Ford coughed once, then settled into rhythm as he turned off the main road. Wipers scraped. For a while he could pretend the world was only weather and not warning. The ledger on the passenger seat disagreed.

He hadn't meant to take it, but the thing had all but asked him to. The leather binding felt brittle, the pages slick with an oily residue that wasn't quite mold. It smelled of iron and ink. Every few miles, it sighed—paper shifting, whispering to itself.

He turned down the radio to be sure. The sound didn't stop.

"Don't start that," he muttered. "Not again."

He reached to shut the ledger though it was already closed. Still, faint scratching continued—pen on paper, too regular to be imagination. Lightning flared across the horizon, and the gilt lettering on the cover burned bright for a second. The name there wasn't Holmes anymore.

It was Gentshaft.

Harold swore softly and snapped it open. The pages were blank except for a fresh line at the top:

Experiment Forty-Three: Observation resumed.

The number chilled him. Forty-three—his great-grandfather's ID in the city archive. Exposure confirmed.

He slammed it shut, dropped it on the floor, and pressed harder on the gas. The highway bent into forest, two lanes of cracked asphalt leading nowhere but the past.

The cabin lay thirty miles north of town, beyond where GPS pretended to know the way. Trees thickened until they formed wet green walls. He rolled the window down, letting pine and rain steady him. The air was sharp, almost antiseptic.

"Figures," he said. "Holmes always liked things sterile."

His reflection in the rearview mirror didn't smile back. For a heartbeat, it wasn't even his face—it was younger, darker, moustache too neat.

Harold blinked hard and the image corrected. The wipers kept time.

He tried the radio again. Static. Beneath it, a faint rhythm—three slow beats, pause, three again. The heartbeat of the ledger.

He turned it off.

The map from city records was useless now; half the roads were ghosts. But he remembered the pattern of the old sewer lines. He'd studied them as an apprentice, chasing rumors of tunnels Holmes had built beneath Chicago, tunnels that were supposed to reach north.

No one believed it.

He did.

He pulled over at mile marker thirty-one, where asphalt ended in gravel. Rain sheeted the windshield, turning the forest beyond into motion. The air smelled faintly of lilies.

He left the engine running and stepped out, flashlight carving thin paths through mist. The ground sloped toward a ravine where the remains of an access tunnel jutted from mud—a brick arch sealed with rusted bolts.

Harold crouched, wiped grime away. A brass plate was set into the keystone. Most letters had worn off, but two words remained: CONTINUITY PROJECT.

"Jesus," he whispered. "They kept it running."

Something shifted behind him—branches or breath. He swung the light. Nothing. Only trees leaning closer.

Then he saw it—a footprint in the mud. Not his. Smaller, recent, half-filled with water.

A woman's boot tread.

So Frank and Julie had been here.

"Still alive then," he murmured. "Still a chance."

He raised his pry bar and went to work. Metal shrieked, echoing too far down the ravine. The sound came back distorted, Morse-like—an answer.

When the last bolt came loose, the door sagged inward. Air rolled out—cold, antiseptic. Harold coughed, eyes watering. The smell was hospital mixed with grave.

He lifted the light. The tunnel beyond was tiled and sweating condensation. Old fixtures hung in ribs along the ceiling, each pulsing with faint gold glow. Not electricity—phosphorescence, like trapped fireflies.

He stepped inside.

Silence swallowed the world. No rain. No wind. Only a low hum, the kind that vibrated behind the eyes.

Halfway down, he found a marking—a triangle drawn in soot, beneath it a date: 1895, and a signature he knew too well.

Martin Gentshaft.

His chest tightened. The neat, deliberate strokes were unmistakable. But beside it another signature slanted in identical style, written in newer ink.

H. H. Holmes.

He'd heard family rumors all his life—Martin Gentshaft, engineer on the Chicago fair, paid in cash and silence. He'd dismissed them. Now he felt the lie rooting itself in his ribs.

"Goddamn it," he whispered. "He had help."

He walked on. The tunnel curved deeper, past collapsed sections and puddles mirroring his light. The hum thickened until it felt alive.

At the next junction he found modern intrusion—city inspection crates stamped with recent logos. Someone else had been down here. The top box lay open. Inside: tools, a Geiger counter, a blinking camera.

He picked it up. The last video played automatically—a shaky image of tile, then movement. The lens turned toward a wall where condensation gathered in patterns. Letters formed through the fog:

Julie S.—termination confirmed.

The feed died.

"Not on my watch," Harold said, though his voice quavered.

He turned toward the next passage. The hum shifted key—lower, almost a pulse. A voice drifted through the damp.

"You came back, Harold."

He froze. "Frank?"

No reply. Only hiss and echo. Then again, nearer: "You were always meant to finish his work."

He swept the beam across the wall. The soot markings bled, shapes reforming into text that hadn't existed seconds ago:

Experiment Forty-Four: Observation resumed.
Subject H.G.—exposure imminent.

Harold's stomach turned to ice. "Like hell."

He backed up—but the way behind him was gone. The tunnel wall had healed over, seamless as flesh.

The hum rose, a living frequency.

"Holmes," he said, forcing calm. "You're memory. Ink and whispers. You can't write me in."

The answer came from everywhere, precise and polite.

You've already signed, Harold. Family tradition.

He looked down. The ledger had opened itself inside his bag, pages turning fast. Ink bled in sharp, surgical lines. His name at the top.

He slammed the bag shut and ran.

The walls narrowed, sweating light. Every few yards, glass panels gleamed—each containing a face, pale and open-eyed. One mouth moved.

Harold.

He sprinted faster.

The tunnel widened into a chamber filled with broken machinery—pipes, tables, rusted tools. An inspection lamp still burned, powered by nothing. Beneath it, a plaque read:

SECTION C—ARCHIVE CORRIDOR.

He crouched, gasping. "Still breathing."

A pause. Only his heartbeat.

Then—quiet. The kind that listens.

He held still. Even the hum seemed to inhale. In that breathless gap he thought he heard something small and melodic—three notes, almost a lullaby. The one Pearl had hummed in the kitchen while helping her mother bake. The melody circled faintly through the pipes.

His skin crawled.

Then the light shifted, stretching his shadow across the wall. The silhouette that rose behind it wasn't his. It was taller. Bowler hat.

Harold turned slowly. The reflection in a steel table smiled with someone else's mouth.

"You're early," it said. "But not unexpected."

The flashlight flickered.

"What do you want?" Harold managed.

"To finish the record," the voice said. "Your family built the foundation. You'll help me preserve it."

The hum deepened, mechanical yet human.

Harold's hand found his lighter. Flame caught—a fragile island of light. The chamber was empty again. No reflection. No hat. Just dripping water.

He exhaled. "Still got it," he muttered.

Then the ledger opened by itself. Letters glowed gold across the page.

Experiment Forty-Five: Subject H.G.—alignment achieved.

The flame died.

Darkness breathed back. The hum filled it, dense and steady, like the sound of lungs filling with water.

A whisper brushed his ear. "Welcome back to the record, Harold."

He didn't remember the scream—only the echo of the ledger closing itself, polite as a librarian shelving a book.

Far above the tunnels, morning struggled through the pines. The cabin's windows glowed weakly against the fog.

Frank woke first. The house was quiet except for the faint vibration underfoot—a low, rhythmic hum.

Julie stirred on the couch, clutching her mother's scarf. "Dad?"

He glanced at the ceiling. "You hear that?"

"The heartbeat again," she whispered.

Outside, fog coiled around the trees like smoke. Somewhere beneath the ground, the same hum pulsed in time with theirs—slow, deliberate, patient.

Frank took her hand. "It's not over."

"No," she said softly. "It's starting again."

The air smelled faintly of lilies.

And far below, in the dark, the ledger turned one more page.

7
The Heart of the House

The rain had thinned to a mist—the kind that erased sound without cleaning anything.

Inside the cabin, everything quivered. Not from the generator, but from the walls themselves. The vibration had rhythm, a living pulse that echoed breath.

Frank sat at the table, fingertips pressed to the grain, searching for something ordinary: the pulse of wood, the faint tremor of wind.

Julie stood by the window, eyes half-closed, face bleached by gray light. She hadn't spoken in nearly an hour.

"Julie," he said softly. "You're scaring me, kiddo."

She blinked once. When she turned, her pupils had tightened to fine points. "He's listening."

"Who?"

"The one beneath."

Frank's mouth went dry. "Holmes?"

She tilted her head slightly, as if hearing a name that had outlived its body. "He prefers continuity. Holmes was just the body."

Frank exhaled through his teeth. "You need to sleep. You're starting to sound like the house."

She smiled faintly. "Maybe the house finally sounds like me."

Before he could answer, the ledger on the table shuddered. It had been there since morning—the same one Harold found in the tunnels, its leather blackened and cold to the touch. Frank hadn't opened it. He'd promised himself he wouldn't.

Now the covers flexed, as though something beneath the paper exhaled.

Julie's gaze sharpened. "He's back."

Frank grabbed the ledger and held it shut. "No, he's not. He's gone."

The pages turned anyway, riffling in a wind that wasn't there. Ink seeped through from inside—black into gold—forming new lines that crawled across the paper.

Experiment 45 – Observer H. Gentshaft – Continuity Breach.

Frank froze. "Harold?"

Julie stepped closer. "He's writing to us."

The words kept forming, the ink pulsing like a heartbeat:

Frank, if you can see this, I made it through. The tunnel under the city leads here. You have to destroy the heart.

Frank's breath hitched. "Jesus, Harold..."

Julie traced the glowing line with her fingertip. "He's in the ledger. Not dead—transcribed."

A slower line appeared, written by a shaking hand:

Holmes built the ledger as a bridge. It records to preserve, but now it feeds. The longer you read, the more it owns you. Don't look away from her. She's the key.

Frank's heartbeat climbed. "What does that mean?"

Julie's lips moved before she answered, as if another voice shaped the syllables. "He means me."

Lightning cracked outside, washing the room in white. When it faded, the writing had changed again:

They copied her rhythm. The house breathes through her now. If it stops, the record stops. Make it stop.

Frank slammed the book shut, but the words glowed through the leather like fireflies beneath skin.

The walls trembled with a low resonance—steady, mechanical, almost human. The heartbeat of the house.

Julie staggered backward, pressing a hand to her chest. "He's merging them," she gasped. "Harold... and the doctor."

Frank caught her shoulders. "Stay with me. Look at me."

Her eyes flicked toward the ledger. "He's still writing."

The book trembled again, opened itself, and a final line etched across the page in frantic strokes:

If you can hear me—burn it. Please.

The ink spread until the letters dissolved into smoke.

Frank yanked the book off the table and hurled it into the fireplace. Flames roared, violent and bright. For a moment, he thought it was over.

Then the fire changed color—gold bleeding into black, smoke curling in spirals that twisted into handwriting midair.

The letters formed Harold's voice through the crackle.

"Frank... I thought I could control it. I was wrong."

"Harold!" Frank shouted. "Where are you?"

The flames answered with an image: a corridor lined with tile, water dripping from the ceiling. Harold stood in the center, face lit by faint gold, the ledger clutched in his hands. Behind him, the walls breathed.

Julie stepped closer, eyes wide. "He's inside the record."

Harold's image turned toward her. "Julie, listen. The ledger connects every version of the house—Chicago, the hospital, this cabin. It's one machine, built to repeat observation. Holmes isn't haunting you. He's editing you."

The flames hissed. Part of Harold's face blurred, replaced by shifting symbols. "If you stop reading, it loses form," he said. "You have to unwrite it."

Julie's breath quickened. "How?"

"Through me," Harold said. "I can hold it long enough. But when it comes, don't let it use my name."

Frank reached toward the fire. "You can't fight him alone—"

The image flared bright. Harold's expression twisted, his voice dropping into something colder. "I'm not alone."

Then the flames went out.

Silence dropped like a shroud. The smell of ozone lingered, laced with faint lilies and phenol.

Julie whispered, "He's part of it now."

The ledger, half-charred, lay in the ashes. Smoke curled from its spine. A single line of gold ink burned through the cover:

Experiment 46 – Integration Successful.

Frank's stomach turned. "He warned us too late."

The walls shuddered. Dust rained from the rafters. Outside, trees swayed though the air was still. The tone deepened into a vibration that rattled their teeth.

Julie clutched her chest. "He's trying to finish the chapter."

Frank caught her as she fell. The floor pulsed beneath them like skin stretched over something alive. The burned ledger flipped open, pages moving in time with the rhythm.

Across the nearest page, Harold's handwriting returned—now split, two voices overlapping:

Destroy the heart / Preserve continuity.

Julie gasped. "They're fighting each other."

Frank ground out the words. "Then we help Harold win."

He grabbed the ledger, ignoring the heat, and hurled it against the wall. The book burst open, scattering pages that drifted like ash. Each one landed writing-side up, pulsing faintly.

Julie pressed a hand to her chest. "It's syncing with my heartbeat."

The ink thickened, forming veins that reached for her feet. Frank swept her off the floor just as the nearest page ignited. Black fire raced outward, drawing a ring around them.

"Julie, stay awake!"

Her eyes flew open, pupils glowing gold. "He's rewriting through me."

"Then reshape him back!"

She clutched his arm, voice trembling. "He says the house remembers everything. We just have to make it forget."

"How?"

"Erase the witness."

The walls rippled, swelling like lungs. Harold's voice broke through again, static and plea: "Frank... the basement. The pulse is there. End it."

Then Holmes's voice answered, smooth and patient: "Observation cannot end, only resume."

Every window shattered inward. Wind and rain burst through, carrying ash and ink. The pages rose, spiraling through the room, each flashing scenes—Holmes's eyes, the tunnels, Julie's death—every experiment looping endlessly.

Julie screamed, "He's collapsing it!"

Frank seized her hand. "Basement—now!"

They stumbled to the cellar door. Light glowed beneath the stairs—sickly yellow. The vibration grew louder, resonating in their bones.

Halfway down, Julie stopped. "Dad... listen."

Through the roar came a smaller pattern—three beats, pause, three again. Harold's rhythm.

"He's still fighting," Frank said.

They reached the bottom. The cellar pulsed with gold light. In the center, the floor had opened like a wound, revealing a shallow pit lined with tile. The rhythm came from within—steady, mechanical.

The ledger's last intact page drifted down the stairs and settled at the pit's edge. Its ink shimmered once, then shaped new words:

Observation reversed.

Julie knelt, trembling. "He's giving us control."

Frank hesitated. Every instinct screamed he'd been wrong all along—that proof had been his blindness. "If this ends it, we do it together."

She met his eyes. "I understand her now. Julie. She didn't curse him—she tried to record her freedom."

Frank's throat tightened. "Then let's finish her entry."

Julie tore a splinter from the stair rail, dipped it into the ink. As she wrote, the page resisted, the pen stuttering. The air fought her hand, like the world itself refusing to be unwritten.

She pressed harder, forcing each word:

End of experiment. Continuity ceased.

The rhythm faltered. The light guttered. The house inhaled once—then stopped.

From the pit, a whisper rose—Harold's voice, faint but calm. "Good girl."

The golden veins recoiled, retreating into earth like nerves pulling from pain. The glow sank away.

Darkness swallowed everything.

Then Julie exhaled and slumped against her father.

Frank held her, listening. No thrum. No whisper. Only rain—honest, uneven, unmeasured—striking the roof.

The ledger lay still beside them, its pages blank.

Frank touched the cover. "Harold?"

Silence. Cooling leather.

Julie opened her eyes. "He's gone."

He nodded slowly. "He finished the chapter."

They climbed the stairs together. The fire had died, leaving only smoke and the faint scent of burnt paper.

Julie looked back once. "He said not to let it use his name."

"It won't," Frank said quietly. "Not anymore."

Outside, dawn thinned the fog. The forest steamed in pale light, water dripping from every leaf.

They buried the ledger beneath the wet earth behind the cabin, neither speaking. When the last shovelful fell, Frank stood still, waiting for the undertone. None came.

Only a birdcall—a single note that stopped midair, as if listening.

He turned toward the cabin. "Let's go home."

Behind them, deep in the soil, one page of the ledger turned itself over and bled a single word into the ash:

Continue?

The ink faded before the morning sun could find it.

8
The Forest and the Ledger

The forest was different at night—too still, as if the trees were holding their breath. The wind that had carried the rain earlier had gone quiet, leaving only the soft crackle of branches shedding their last drops. Fog drifted low to the ground, hugging roots and stones, turning every shadow into a possible shape.

Julie walked ahead of her father, flashlight trembling in her grip. The beam cut through the mist in pale ribbons, catching the glitter of wet bark. Every step sounded too loud. Every pause, too long.

"Harold?" she whispered. "If you can hear us, we need to understand."

The word understand seemed to echo, but the echo wasn't hers. It came from deeper in the woods, lower, slower, like an imitation spoken a breath too late. Her pulse kicked hard.

Frank caught her arm. "Wait. Did you hear that?"

"I think he's answering."

Frank angled his flashlight into the trees. The beam snagged on nothing. Just fog, endless fog. "Or something else is."

They'd come here because of the dream—the same one both had woken from, hearts hammering, the words help me scrawled in condensation on the cabin window. Harold's name had been written below it in a child's hand.

Julie had known immediately. "He's not gone," she'd said. "He's trying to warn us."

Now, standing in the forest that bordered the cabin, she wasn't so sure. The woods felt alive in a way that made her skin crawl, the air thick with the same hum she'd sworn had ended when they escaped the house. It was softer now, almost tender, like a heartbeat waiting for permission to grow louder.

"Harold," she called again. "You said you'd help us finish this."

A faint rustle answered from the direction of the stream. Then a light—dim, the color of candle flame—flickered between the trunks. It moved slowly, like someone carrying a lantern through fog.

Frank stepped in front of her, one hand outstretched. "Stay behind me."

They moved together, careful, the flashlight beam chasing the glow until it stopped beside an old elm. The light pulsed once, then steadied. Through the haze, Harold Gentshaft stood as if he'd been waiting all along. His outline was intact—hat, coat, the familiar slump of his shoulders—but the air around him shimmered, bending light where it touched him.

"Jesus," Frank whispered. "Harold..."

The ghost smiled faintly. "Don't use that name too loud out here, Frank. He listens for it."

Julie swallowed hard. "We saw your truck—empty. The bridge—"

"I know." Harold's voice sounded wet, distant, like something spoken through rainwater. "I made it halfway across before he remembered me."

"Holmes," Frank said.

The echo smiled wider, and for a second, his face blurred—two images layered: Harold's and another, smoother, colder.

"He prefers Continuity now," Harold said quietly. "Holmes was only the experiment's first name."

Julie stepped closer. The air around him hummed faintly, prickling her skin. "You wanted to help us."

"I did." His expression softened. "Still do. But he found a way to listen through me."

The forest responded with a low vibration that made the leaves shiver. Frank felt it through the soles of his boots. "Then stop talking."

"Too late," Harold murmured. "He's already rewriting."

The lantern-light inside him flared, illuminating the fog. For a heartbeat, Julie saw shapes within it—rooms layered over the forest, corridors where trees should be, metal tables glinting beneath phantom lamps.

She gasped. "It's the house."

Harold nodded slowly. "He's trying to rebuild it through memory. Every place you touch becomes a draft."

Frank's throat tightened. "Then this whole forest—"

"—is paper," Harold finished. "And you're walking on the words."

The fog thickened. Somewhere in the dark, the sound of typewriter keys began—soft, deliberate, uneven. Tap. Tap. Tap. Each strike made the ground tremble a little more.

Julie turned in a slow circle. "What do we do?"

Harold's gaze flicked toward her, and for a moment, it wasn't Harold's at all. The pupils narrowed to perfect black points.

"He wants your eyes," the other voice said through Harold's mouth. "They remember too clearly."

Frank yanked Julie behind him. "You're not Harold."

The echo faltered, flickering like a candle in a draft. "I'm both," it said. "He needs me to find the end."

The words hit Julie like ice. "You can't fight him?"

"I can slow him," Harold said, his tone shifting back to human for a heartbeat. "But you need to go back. The ledger—"

"The ledger?" Frank echoed. "We left it in the truck."

"No," Harold said, voice breaking apart. "It's in the cabin now. He moved it. He wants her to open it."

The light inside him surged, too bright to look at. Julie shielded her eyes. "Harold!"

He reached toward her. His fingers were light, transparent, but she felt the cold brush of them against her cheek.

"You can't destroy him by running," he whispered. "Only by rewriting him."

Then the light went out.

Silence fell so hard it rang. The fog collapsed inward, snuffing itself out like breath against glass. The woods were suddenly empty—no hum, no wind—only the wet, waiting dark.

Frank stayed frozen a moment, the beam of his flashlight steady but shaking in his grip.

He whispered, "Leslie always said observation was empathy, not ownership. Maybe that's what he never understood."

Julie looked at him. His voice had gone small, reverent—something closer to prayer than reason.

He squeezed her shoulder. "Let's go."

They retraced their steps through the dark, half-running, the path warping beneath their boots. Every so often Julie glimpsed

Harold's silhouette between the trees, flickering ahead of them like a guide. By the time the cabin came into view, the mist had vanished, leaving the woods too clean, too sharp, as if someone had erased the blur of distance.

The porch light glowed faintly though neither of them had left it on.

Frank hesitated at the steps. "You sure we want to go back in?"

"We don't have a choice," Julie said. "If the ledger's here, we need to see it before he does."

Her voice wavered, guilt threading through it. "He used me, Dad. I think he still can."

He glanced at her, realizing the fear beneath her control wasn't just terror—it was responsibility. "Then we make sure he never can again."

Inside, the air smelled of ozone and old paper. Everything looked untouched—the scattered books, the kettle, the steno pad on the table—but the light felt wrong, brighter at the edges, dimmer at the center.

Then they saw it. The ledger sat on the table beside the steno pad, its cover damp and gleaming. Water—or something pretending to be it—dripped from the leather, forming small, perfect circles on the wood.

Frank moved closer, careful. "It wasn't here when we left."

Julie touched the edge of the table. Her fingers came away cold. "He's already been through it."

The ledger shuddered once, like something breathing beneath the cover. Then it opened by itself, pages fluttering to the center. Words crawled across the paper—ink forming letters that hadn't been there a second ago.

Observation Resumed. Subject J.S. in situ.

Frank grabbed Julie's hand. "Don't read it."

"It's writing itself," she said, unable to look away. The next line appeared, darker, faster.

External interference detected. H.G. containment failed. Correction in progress.

"Harold," she breathed. "He tried to stop it."

The ledger pulsed. The ink spread across both pages, forming a single shape—a circle divided into sections, each labeled with numbers that didn't stay still. At its center was a symbol Julie recognized: the stylized eye from Holmes's old laboratory records.

Frank slammed the book shut. The cabin lights flickered, then steadied.

"Whatever that thing is," he said, "we're done letting it talk."

But the sound of the typewriter began again—this time not from the woods, but from directly beneath their feet. Slow. Heavy. Measured.

Julie's gaze snapped toward the floorboards. "He's underneath."

The tapping grew louder, syncing perfectly with the rhythm of her heartbeat. Tap. Tap. Tap. Then a pause—long enough for the silence to stretch thin—and another tap, right under her chair.

Frank pulled her back. "Upstairs. Move."

They climbed fast, the old stairs groaning under their weight. The light from below glowed faintly through the cracks, each pulse following them like a living heartbeat. When they reached the landing, Julie stopped short. The mirror on the wall—the same one she'd covered nights ago—was uncovered again.

Her reflection stared back at her, eyes wide, lips moving though she hadn't spoken.

"Dad," she whispered, "look."

The reflection smiled, faint and wrong. Then it lifted its hand, palm outward, pressing against the inside of the glass. Letters appeared on the surface in backward script.

HELP HIM.

Frank moved to pull her away, but the mirror's surface rippled like water, drawing her reflection closer. The glass fogged, forming a second word beneath the first.

HURRY.

The handwriting was Harold's.

Julie's chest tightened. "He's fighting it."

"Or baiting us," Frank said. "Either way, we play this on our terms."

He grabbed the blanket from the banister and threw it over the mirror again. The fabric twitched once, as though something underneath had exhaled.

For a long time, neither of them spoke. The cabin settled into uneasy silence—the kind that felt aware.

Finally Julie whispered, "He said the ledger was the key. If we rewrite him—"

"We'll figure it out in daylight," Frank said. "For now, we keep that book shut."

They moved back to the table together. The ledger sat motionless, its cover perfectly dry now. On its spine, the embossed letters had changed color—from black to faint, shimmering gold.

Frank reached for it, then stopped. "Julie."

She followed his gaze. The condensation where the book had rested had formed words on the wood, faint but legible.

Continuity Maintained.

Julie's voice was barely a breath. "He's still watching."

Frank picked up the book and shoved it into the iron woodstove. The cover hissed when it touched metal, releasing the sharp scent of antiseptic and lilies—sweet and clinical, like memory turned chemical.

"Then let him watch this," he said.

He struck a match. The flame caught instantly, burning blue before turning orange. For a moment, the room glowed warm, ordinary. Julie almost believed it was over.

Then the pages began to scream.

Not loudly, not human, but a high, thin whine like metal bending under impossible pressure. The flames flickered, struggling to consume the paper. The ledger shifted, its spine cracking open like a mouth.

Julie's hands flew to her ears. "Dad!"

He reached for the stove door. "Don't look—"

The fire went out.

Smoke filled the room—cold, gray, reeking of ink. In its center, the ledger sat intact, unburned. The words on its cover had rearranged themselves into a single new line.

Observation Deferred.

Frank stared at it, chest heaving. "It means we bought time."

The smoke thinned slowly. Through it, Julie thought she saw movement—a figure standing just beyond the cabin door, watching. The shape was tall, familiar. A hat brim. A coat.

"Harold?" she whispered.

The figure tilted its head once, then dissolved into fog.

The silence that followed was neither peace nor threat—just breath held by the world itself, waiting to see what they would write next.

9

INHERITANCE

Rain followed them into the city, tracing the truck's side mirrors like veins. Streetlights smeared into milky halos, and the slick roads doubled themselves—thin as memories laid over glass. Frank's hands held at ten and two, the way he drove when he needed control. He'd run this stretch too many times to be lost, but the geometry felt wrong—angles a degree longer, corners drawn with a heavier hand.

The radio murmured low static, almost breathing. He turned the dial until it clicked home. Silence followed, and still the quiet thrummed.

Julie kept her gaze on the post office ahead—ordinary red brick, ordinary glass doors. Ordinary until you remembered what lay beneath. Corridors paved over. Bones filed under letters and packages. History pretending to be civilized. Her throat ached from dreams she couldn't close. There had been a beaker once, curved and wrong, catching her face while someone wiped its rim and called her Julia—as if the name were permission.

She gripped the knife in her lap, one from Frank's old field kit—a practical tool until last week, when it began reflecting what wasn't there. The steel caught the weak morning light and threw it across the dashboard in a trembling ribbon. She tilted it a fraction, and the ribbon narrowed into a band that behaved less like light and more like a gaze.

Frank glanced over. "Where'd you even get that thing again?"

"It was in the evidence box you kept from the estate sale," she said.

He frowned. "I thought those were just old tools."

"They were," she murmured, turning the blade. Near the hilt, faint letters surfaced through the rust—H.H., followed by a string of numbers.

"It's from the Castle," Harold's voice came faintly from the radio. "Police auctioned off the evidence decades ago. Some pieces never made it to storage."

A chill climbed her wrist. "Then it's already part of his story."

"Maybe that's why it can show him," Harold added. "A mirror that remembers."

Holmes's reflection surfaced in the blade—eyes bright as coin, mouth wearing that small, courtly smile that made pain seem polite.

She blinked. The knife showed only her knuckles, slick with sweat.

"Leave it in the truck," Frank said quietly.

"I might need it."

"For what?"

She hesitated. "For me."

He looked at her, really looked, as if his eyes could hold her when his hands could not. Somewhere, a siren wailed and broke apart. He didn't ask again.

They parked where the asphalt collected water in shallow mirrors. The post office sat squat against the sky—just another box for sorting names. A brass plaque gleamed green at the edges like an old wound.

Julie stepped out. The air smelled of wet paper and antiseptic—the ghost scent that had followed them since the cabin. The automatic door parted with a polite sigh. Fluorescents buzzed overhead, a pale mimicry of the undertone she still felt in her bones.

The knife glinted once more. The reflection returned, closer this time, smiling wider.

Inside, the air was colder than it should have been. The machine-breath of the vents carried something slower underneath—a respiration too steady to be human. Tile stretched ahead, polished to a mirror sheen. Her reflection pooled beneath her boots, elongated, thin as water.

Frank kept his voice measured. "Ten minutes. Then we're done."

She nodded, but her feet were already turning toward the corridor marked EMPLOYEES ONLY. The undertone deepened, threading through her ribs. Each step woke something buried under her skin—rooms remembered, straps tightening, the precise chill of chloroform.

You remember the halls, a voice murmured. Not a voice—breath shaped to sound, close enough to fog her ear.

Her pulse stuttered. "No," she said aloud. "I don't."

The blade shimmered again, and Holmes appeared—assembled from silver, eyes kind enough to lie. His reflection moved half a beat behind hers, as if the distance had been measured and preserved.

THE DEVIL INSIDE

Welcome home, said the smile.

The overhead light flickered. Tile whispered under her boots. Behind the wall, something sighed, and lilies sweetened the air.

"Jules?" Frank called. "You okay?"

She opened her mouth, but her reflection smiled first. The knife didn't show her teeth; it showed his.

The corridor shifted as she blinked—same shape, different century. Wood replaced tile. Gas hissed from unseen pipes. The air thickened, heavy with intent. Gaslight breathed along the walls like an organism pretending to be architecture.

She took one step forward. Her boots thudded on plank instead of stone.

In the knife's reflection, Holmes stood at her shoulder, serene.

You feel it now, don't you? The pulse. The inheritance.

Her stomach tightened at the word. She said nothing. Naming gave it form.

Frank saw only his daughter held mid-step, blade angled toward her reflection. His chest locked, but he didn't rush her. "Julie," he said gently. "Put the knife down."

She didn't move.

To her, the corridor ran forever—doorways opening into other decades, voices rippling thin and constant as dripping water. Somewhere, a woman cried a name that could have been hers. Julia.

Holmes leaned closer in the blade, whispering, You called me back.

"No," she breathed, though it fogged the air.

Every name is an invitation, he said.

Behind her, Frank edged closer. The fluorescent whine rose to meet him. "Jules, look at me. You're here."

She flicked her eyes toward his voice—and for a heartbeat, two centuries overlapped. Holmes turned with her, his gaze aligning perfectly through hers.

For a fraction of a second, Frank saw both: his daughter and the echo overlaid, another mouth moving one frame late. "Jules?" His own name felt wrong in his throat.

She lifted the knife slowly, reverently. In the reflection, another hand lifted too—a man's, sure and steady. Every instinct screamed, but Frank stayed still.

"You're here," he said again. "Stay with me."

The temperature plunged. Frost veined the walls. His breath fogged white. Her eyes darkened to ink. The undertone pressed against their hearts.

Then she slashed—not at him, but sideways, cutting air at an impossible angle.

The sound wasn't metal through space. It was glass breaking without noise.

Light bent. Reality rippled like heat.

For an instant, he saw it—the corridor beneath the corridor: gaslight, tiled walls, instruments gleaming. Holmes's laboratory overlaid on the modern floor. Julie stood in both worlds.

Then it vanished.

She blinked, grip slackening. The knife tip kissed tile. "Dad?"

He was already there. He caught her, the cold in her skin shocking his palms. Her weight folded into him. Her pulse fluttered—too slow, learning again.

"Breathe," he whispered. "Come back."

Her eyes opened halfway, green but shadowed. Something passed behind them—a ripple darker than sight.

"Stay with me," he said.

She inhaled. The sound doubled—two voices sharing one throat. Beneath their feet, the floor answered with a low thud, followed by a sigh like pressure releasing.

He looked down. Water shimmered over the tiles, showing faint lines beneath—arches, hallways, the ghost of a building remembered too well.

Julie's hand twitched toward it. "He's waiting."

"Who?"

"You know."

A metallic clink echoed—scalpel to tray, polite as punctuation. The sweetness of chloroform deepened.

He helped her stand. "We're leaving."

She didn't fight, but her eyes lingered on the wet floor. "He's underneath. The floor remembers."

Vibration climbed through their shoes, gentle as a heartbeat and sure as intent. Envelopes slipped from cubbies and drifted into the air, pale birds startled from hiding.

Frank held her tighter. "Almost there."

At the door, the lights flickered. For a heartbeat, his reflection wore Holmes's smile. He didn't tell her.

Outside, rain washed everything clean but sound. They stepped into it together. The knife gleamed at her side. Behind them, the post office dimmed its lights one by one, like a house exhaling.

Rain beaded on the truck's hood like sweat on cooling skin. He opened the door for her, guiding her in. The blade took the sodium light, turning its edge the color of gold gone old.

"You're okay," he said, maybe to both of them.

Inside, the silence hummed. Wipers marked time.

Julie's voice came small. "He's not sleeping."

"Who?"

She turned the knife. The reflection inside wasn't theirs. It moved—a man's head turning, a smile too kind.

"Jesus," Frank whispered.

Holmes blinked. The motion rippled through the steel like breath over water.

"He followed," she said.

"It's a trick," he muttered. "Refraction."

She laughed without humor. "Refraction doesn't breathe."

Condensation bloomed on the windshield—one handprint, perfect and still.

Frank slammed the truck into gear. Tires hissed. The post office shrank behind them until it was only shadow.

Still, the air inside smelled of antiseptic and lilies. Holmes rode with them, quiet and patient.

Julie stared at her reflection. "He said walls remember. What if the body does too?"

He didn't answer. The road ahead doubled again. Beside her, the knife shimmered with motion. The undertone returned—not from a building, but from within.

The motel waited on the city's edge, a tired row beneath a flickering sign promising CLEAN ROOMS. Frank pulled in, gravel crunching. The thrum sank low, into their bones.

He killed the engine. "Stay here."

She nodded but watched the knife. It fogged once, then cleared.

Inside the blur, shapes shifted—three silhouettes, one smiling.

He came back dripping rain. "Room eight." He caught her clutching the knife like prayer. "It's just a room, Jules. Four walls. That's all."

Inside, bleach and carpet. The air thickened instantly. Frank set the knife on the dresser. "Out of your hand," he said gently. "You need rest."

She obeyed, sitting on the bed. The mirror opposite caught them both—and something else. A third outline behind her, tall, patient, a hand resting on her shoulder.

"Jules," Frank said quietly. "Don't move."

Her reflection turned first.

The figure smiled—a practiced expression. Then the glass cleared, leaving only their tired faces.

"Just reflection," he lied.

Behind them, the knife gleamed. Three figures now. The third still smiling.

Sometime after midnight, whispering pulled him from half-sleep. Julie sat by the dresser, the knife upright against her knees, light trembling across her face.

"Jules?"

She didn't turn. The whispers rolled, rhythmic, two voices sharing one breath.

He rose slowly. "Who are you talking to?"

She tilted her head. "You don't have to be afraid, Frank. I can see the symmetry now."

"That's not you."

"He says fear is the first cut," she said softly. "Once it's made, everything opens."

"Step away from the knife."

"I can't. He's showing me what's underneath."

The air turned to ice. Frost veined the mirror. In the blade, Holmes's face settled over hers, lips moving with her own.

Frank lunged, grabbing the handle. The metal burned cold. "Let go!"

She looked up—eyes half hers, half not. "He's almost finished."

The bulb overhead shattered. Darkness folded the room.

He hurled the knife into the sink. Porcelain cracked. Sound snapped the spell.

Julie collapsed forward, gasping.

He caught her, heart hammering. "You're okay."

Her eyes fluttered. "He's not in the walls anymore," she whispered. "He's in me."

He held her until the tremor eased.

From the sink came a slow drip—three drops, pause, three again. The rhythm was wrong enough to be deliberate.

He turned. The knife lay across the basin. Light found its edge. Holmes stared back, patient as ever.

Julie's reflection appeared in the glass—upright, wrong, smiling.

"You opened the door," it said.

He stepped forward. "Julie?"

The smile refined. "She invited me. You confirmed it."

The mirror fogged, veins racing across its surface like lungs. "Get out of her," he said.

The glass cracked, sighing.

"Frank," came Julie's real voice from behind him, "he's in the mirror. He says there's room for two."

He slammed a towel into the glass. Crack. Crack. Relief. Shards scattered into the sink, catching light like tiny mirrors.

Silence.

Then water surged, carrying fragments into the drain. In each one, a reflection blinked awake—a hundred miniature Holmeses, each smiling.

Every surface answered—the TV, the doorknob, the chrome handle—each learning to breathe.

"He said mirrors were only practice," Julie whispered. "Now they're windows."

Her feet left frost on the carpet. Each reflection copied her differently—some scared, some smiling, one with his eyes.

He grabbed her wrist. "Don't look."

The shards clicked like teeth. From every surface, his name whispered.

They ran.

Outside, rain washed glass into the gutter. Every window blinked once—light, dark, light—as if the city were learning sight.

They drove in silence. Rain flattened everything into ribbons. Headlights cut tunnels through the dark.

"Where are we going?" she asked.

"Someplace dry. Far from mirrors."

The radio crackled alive. Static matched the wipers' time. He reached for the dial, but it spun free.

Frank.

He froze.

"You heard it too," she said.

He twisted it down. The undertone sank lower—into metal, into bone.

"Don't listen," he warned.

You changed the frame, the speaker replied, pleased.

He slammed the dash. The radio squealed, then searched. A waltz emerged—warped, slow. Beneath it, another sound: breathing.

"He's learning our rhythm," Julie whispered.

The dial moved on its own. Between static: Catalogued... viable... Julie S.—termination confirmed.

He hit the radio until his hand ached. Silence—almost.

Lightning flared. In its flash, another mouth moved under her skin.

"Dad," she whispered. "He's in the signal now."

He pulled onto the shoulder. Gravel spat. Rain hammered. His hand went to the dial.

"Don't," she warned.

It spun faster—voices overlapping.

Experiment Twelve: Julie S.—termination confirmed.

He flinched. The lights flickered red, then green.

Experiment Thirteen: Subject J—parameters consistent.

Julie pressed her palms to her head. "He's cataloging us."

"Jules—"

Her tone split. "Fourteen. Subject remains compliant. Tissue responds."

He shook her. "That's not you!"

Her voice overlapped his: "Fifteen. Behavioral variance increasing. Possible attachment."

The undertone purred approval.

He ripped the radio free and threw it into the rain. Sparks died in the gutter.

Silence.

"Dad?" she said softly. "Where's the radio?"

"In a ditch," he breathed. "It's over."

But it wasn't. The thrum returned, soft as breath. Her pupils tightened. "He says you can't destroy what's already inside."

He gripped the wheel. "We're done listening."

"You never stop," she said. "That's how he learns."

Lightning flashed again, turning the world negative. Holmes's face overlaid hers for one perfect instant.

Then darkness took the rest.

The hum followed them down the road—low, patient, alive.

Back in the ditch, the ruined radio flickered green. Inside its broken speaker, a man's voice whispered one last line, calm and certain:

Experiment Eighteen: environment receptive. Continuation assured.

Rain swallowed the sound. The night learned a new rhythm.

10

The Bone Ledger

The rain came down like needles—thin, sharp, unrelenting—making the world shimmer and hiss. Frank's hands locked at ten and two, shoulders tight. The wipers beat a stubborn rhythm, trying to hold a line. Beside him, Julie's reflection fractured in the windshield—two eyes, two faces, neither steady.

The road gleamed black and endless.

Then the radio clicked on by itself.

Static filled the cab—dry, patient. Beneath it, a pulse. Julie's heartbeat answered before she could stop it. The sound wasn't random. It was measured.

"Frank..."

Weak. Distorted through interference. Familiar.

"Frank, you there?"

Frank's jaw hardened. "Harold?"

The static deepened into breath. "Couldn't stay gone," the voice said, cracking on the last word. "Ledger wasn't finished."

Julie turned, low-voiced. "Dad, that's impossible. He's—"

"Dead, I know." Frank stared ahead; his voice wavered anyway. "That's his voice."

The cab filled with a smell—lemon cleaner, paper, dust—the ghost of Harold's store. Rain traced crooked veins across the glass. Harold's voice came again, closer now, almost inside the truck.

"Don't let him write again. He uses what's left of us for ink."

The radio popped once, twice. Silence.

Then the faint scratch of pen on paper.

Julie pressed her palms to her ears. "He's in there," she whispered. "In the signal."

Frank veered onto the shoulder, gravel spitting. "If that's really Harold, he's trying to finish what he started."

"Or lure us back," Julie said, meeting his eyes. "You know where."

The radio whispered again—softer, trembling.

"Ledger's the key. Pages still moving. Bring the knife. It remembers her name."

The engine coughed and died. Dashboard lights blinked out. For a moment the only glow came from the knife in Julie's lap—its blade pulsing, faint as a fingertip over a vein.

Frank's voice went reverent. "He wants us to finish it."

Julie stared at the blade. "Or he wants out."

The post office rose from fog like a mausoleum pretending at normal. Red brick slick with rain. Windows dark, unreflective. Parking lot lights buzzing—the same thin undertone that had haunted the house.

Frank stepped out first. The rain stopped as if it had been waiting.

Inside, the air smelled of ozone and something too clean. A wet trail led from the threshold to the back hallway, each footprint shallow, evaporating as they watched. He followed it to the counter. The vinyl dipped under his boot.

Julie spoke softly. "It's hollow."

He crouched and found the seam by touch—a trapdoor beneath layers of linoleum. "Harold said there was one," he murmured. "Old service tunnel."

Julie knelt beside him. "Dad, don't—"

The lights dimmed, flickering amber. The undertone rose from the foundation like something remembering its own rhythm. He lifted the trapdoor. Cold air sighed up, smelling of rust and lilies.

A narrow spiral of stairs waited below.

Frank glanced at her. "Stay close."

The steps were slick; brick walls sweated condensation. The thrum grew louder with every turn, an undercurrent they felt in their teeth. When his boots met concrete, he stopped.

The chamber looked alive.

A desk stood in the center, wood dark with wet ink. An open ledger lay atop it, pages fluttering though no draft moved. The air wavered like heat over asphalt.

Frank stepped closer. "Harold?"

The ledger stilled. A single word wrote itself across the page in gold-black:

CONTINUITY RESUMED.

Julie's breath caught. "Dad, don't touch—"

Another line surfaced beneath, bleeding through like veins under skin:

FRANKLIN SIMMONS — OBSERVATION REOPENED.

The pitch climbed. Frank stumbled back, clutching his hand—black lines snaking up his wrist like burns. "It's reading me."

THE DEVIL INSIDE

Julie's voice broke. "Not reading. Writing you."

Ink trembled; air behind the desk folded inward. Harold's face flickered into view—thin, gray, eyes hollow. He raised a trembling hand as if to apologize. Then the image lengthened and smoothed into something else.

A dark coat. A bowler hat. A faint, deliberate smile.

Holmes.

"You brought the knife," he said softly, lips not moving. "Good. The instrument completes the record."

Julie lifted the blade. "You're only memory."

His eyes gleamed. "And memory never dies."

Pages turned themselves. Faster. The motion blurred—a whirl of black and gold ink. Smell of old paper and gas. Ribbons of liquid script spun up the walls. Wherever they touched, faces bloomed—pale, half-made, eyes shifting. Harold among them. Others, long gone.

Frank lunged for the ledger. "Then we end the record!"

He slammed his palm down. Pain traveled through his arm—cold as mercury. Letters branded his skin:

SUBJECT F — PENDING RECORD.

"Dad!" Julie slashed the knife through one ink ribbon. It shrieked—metal torn without metal—and burst to sparks.

Holmes didn't flinch. "You can't cut continuity. It shifts."

Julie's hand found the oil lamp on the desk. "Maybe not thought," she said, voice shaking. "But paper burns."

She hurled the lamp.

Fire took the ledger.

Ink screamed.

Flame poured upward, pale at its core, bending light into shapes. Faces shriveled, dissolved. Harold's voice broke through—weak, human. "Finish it, Frank... before he writes you too!"

Ether stung their throats. Pages lifted like wings, tearing free. Each disintegrated to ash midair—each face fading with it.

Silence fell.

"It's over," Julie gasped. "It's—"

A voice rose from the smoke, calm, composed. "Fire doesn't destroy record, Julie. It merely edits."

Holmes stepped through the ash. His outline glowed. Hat brim perfect. Patient smile intact.

Frank snatched a metal stool and swung. It passed through him like smoke.

"You're not real!"

"Reality is consistency," Holmes said mildly. "You've provided both."

The fire collapsed, drawn down into cracks opening like veins. Light drained through, leaving a low glow under the floor.

Julie knelt, palm to stone. The undertone returned—louder, mechanical. "Dad," she whispered. "It's underneath."

The fissure widened, spilling light like molten glass.

Holmes laughed. "You can't burn a foundation, Franklin. Only expose what it supports."

A stair spiraled down beneath them.

The air below was heavy and sweet. Glass cylinders lined the walls—hundreds—filled with pale fluid that glowed from within. Floating inside: scraps of paper, fragments of bone, sometimes both. They pulsed softly, in time. The sound became a living heartbeat.

Julie stared, horrified. "It's not a ledger anymore. It's a body."

Frank wiped condensation from one cylinder. Words drifted up inside:

Subject H.G. — Partial Restoration Achieved.

He stumbled back. "Harold…"

Holmes's voice echoed from deeper in.

"Not restoration. Preservation."

He stood among the cylinders, coat immaculate, hands clasped. "History forgets. I correct its error."

"You murdered to study," Frank said.

Holmes smiled faintly. "I refined them. They live perfectly here, unchanging. Continuity eternal."

Julie's voice thinned. "You turned memory into an organism."

His gaze flicked to her. "Every scientist admires their best subject."

The glow intensified. The vibration became physical, rattling bone and thought. Julie clutched her temples, teeth set. "He's in all of them!"

"Then we break them!" Frank shouted.

He grabbed a valve and twisted. Glass split; glowing liquid hissed across the floor. Another valve—another crack—another body released. Faces blurred to steam.

Holmes's composure faltered. "You're undoing progress."

"That's the idea," Frank growled, smashing a cylinder with the wrench from his belt.

Julie drove the knife into a seam. Cracks webbed outward, bright. One by one, the cylinders ruptured, flooding the chamber in waves of burning white.

Holmes's eyes flared. "Erasure breeds return."

"Then let's see how fast you come back," Julie said, and plunged the knife into the glowing seam of the floor.

The sound that followed was the earth screaming—low, endless. Gold surged up, swallowing Holmes, the walls, the air.

White.

Then nothing.

They woke on cold stone. The air held ash and dust. Blank walls. No undertone.

Julie sat up first. "Dad?"

He coughed. "Still here."

At the room's center: what remained of the ledger—charred, smoking. Beside it, untouched by flame, a smaller book lay whole. Its leather gleamed faintly gold.

Julie lifted it.

The Bone Ledger.

Inside, the first line was written in neat black ink:

Observation continued — Harold Gentshaft.

Frank's throat tightened. "He made his own copy."

"Or he saved us in his," she said quietly.

He thumbed the blank pages. "Either way, it's unfinished."

On the old ledger's last intact page, new words shimmered, then thinned:

Experiment concluded. Subject released.

Julie exhaled. "We should leave before this place remembers us."

They climbed. Dawn bled through the front windows. The post office looked ordinary again. Empty. Harmless.

A single envelope lay on the counter, ink black and spidery:

To Harold Gentshaft — Return to Sender.

Frank didn't touch it.

Outside, the rain had stopped. Streets steamed in new light. Julie slid The Bone Ledger into her pack. "If it's blank, maybe it's waiting for something better."

"Or someone," Frank said, starting the engine.

The truck rolled forward. Sunlight took the windows behind them, and for one heartbeat every pane turned gold.

Then clear.

Beneath the floor, a faint undertone restarted—soft, patient, endless.

Among the ashes, a single line rewrote itself in clean, perfect script:

Observation deferred. Awaiting new witness.

The light dimmed.

The ledger exhaled once, satisfied.

Above, the morning went on pretending nothing had happened.

11
The Inheritance of Echoes

They drove until the city thinned into warehouse lots and silent overpasses. Dawn came hesitant, bleeding through cloud and exhaust. Julie watched it through the windshield, the Bone Ledger balanced on her knees like a living thing. Its cover drank light instead of reflecting it, a black so complete it seemed to pull color from the world.

Frank's hands stayed locked at ten and two, jaw tight enough to ache. Every time he blinked, Harold's face appeared in the rearview—lit by fire, eyes calm in the way that only meant surrender. It should have comforted him. It didn't.

"Say something," he muttered finally.

Julie didn't look up. "What would you like me to say? That it's over?"

The ledger's edges pulsed faintly beneath her fingers. "It doesn't feel over."

Frank exhaled hard through his nose. "Maybe that's just nerves."

"No," she said, barely audible over the engine. "It's breathing."

He risked a glance. The pages inside the ledger rose and fell—subtle, rhythmic, like lungs learning restraint. He reached for it, but she pulled away.

"Don't," she warned. "He listens through contact."

"Who does?"

"Harold," she said, and then—after a beat too long—"and him."

Frank stared. "You're hearing Harold again?"

Julie nodded. "He says there's one more place. Holmes's first lab. Under the old City Hall. The fire never touched it. That's where the last experiment waits."

"Experiment?"

She opened the ledger. The first page was no longer blank. Faint ink bled through from beneath the paper, words that hadn't existed hours ago.

The Inheritance – Final transcription pending.

Frank swallowed. "Jesus Christ."

Julie tilted her head. "He's listening when we use that name."

He gripped the wheel tighter. "Then let him."

They reached the edge of the lake just as sunlight broke through the clouds, pale and uncertain. Frank parked beneath a maple leaning half-dead toward the water. The air smelled of wet iron and old ash, the ghost of a city still learning to cool. He turned off the ignition, letting the ticking engine fill the silence. The reflection of the trees on the water trembled as if the lake itself were trying to breathe.

"All right," he said finally. "Start from the top."

Julie's hands shook when she turned the ledger toward him. "He said Holmes was studying the afterlife. Not heaven or hell—continuity. What happens when consciousness refuses to stop."

"And Harold told you this?"

"Through the ledger. Through memory." She closed her eyes. "He says we're still in the experiment."

Frank rubbed at his eyes. "Jesus, Jules, he's dead."

"He's information now," she said softly. "And information doesn't die."

He wanted to argue, to drag them both back toward science, but the ground beneath the car gave a small, hollow thud—three beats, then stillness. He froze.

"Did you feel—"

"Heartbeat," Julie finished. "He's mapping through us."

The motel they found near the water was the kind of place that had been old even in the eighties: brown curtains, a dead vending machine, a front desk that smelled like bleach and sleep. The clerk barely looked up, his eyes gray and too tired to register the century.

Room 6 held two narrow beds and a table scarred with cigarette burns. Julie set the ledger on it like an offering. Frank checked the locks twice.

"If it's a network like you think," he said, "maybe we can sever it. Electricity, radio waves—something physical."

She shook her head. "It's narrative, not signal. He exists wherever someone tries to understand him."

Frank stared. "And you want to keep reading."

"Harold says we have to. Otherwise the story loops."

The desk phone rang.

They both froze. No one had the number.

Frank picked it up slowly. "Hello?"

For a moment, nothing but static—then Harold's voice, thin but certain. "Frank. Listen to me."

Frank's throat tightened. "Harold?"

"You have to finish the ledger," the voice said. "He's rewriting through you. The pages are memory—Holmes's and yours."

"What does he want?"

"To become continuity itself. To live inside observation."

The line crackled. Julie moved closer, her hand hovering above the receiver. "Harold," she said, "how do we stop him?"

"You don't," Harold whispered. "You replace him."

The phone clicked dead.

That night, Julie couldn't sleep. She dreamed in fragments: the lake glass-smooth, Harold's reflection breaking the surface. His mouth formed words she couldn't hear. Behind him, Holmes smiled with borrowed calm, like a man teaching a ghost how to breathe.

When she woke, the ledger lay open on her chest. New writing covered both pages in a hand that wasn't hers.

Observer accepted. Specimen compliant. Inheritance transferring.

She whispered, "No," but the ink shimmered and sank into the paper like breath being swallowed.

Frank stirred beside her. "Another dream?"

"More like a reminder," she said. "He's updating the record."

He sat up, rubbing the back of his neck. "Then we burn it."

"I told you—it doesn't burn. Harold tried."

"Then we tear it apart, page by page."

She met his eyes. "And lose Harold with it?"

Frank stopped. The answer was written across her face before he asked the question.

By afternoon the sky had gone gray again. Rain pressed against the windows in soft, rhythmic taps. Julie turned the ledger open, studying the way the ink had changed—less written, more grown. Small veins of black threaded outward like roots seeking soil. The smell of ozone returned, faint and familiar, the scent of old experiments waking up.

Frank busied himself by dismantling the motel clock radio. He told himself it was for distraction; he couldn't admit it was for control.

"Electricity carries him," Julie said quietly. "You're not wrong. It's just that we're better conductors."

He looked at her. "You don't sound like yourself."

"Maybe this is myself. The part he couldn't write."

"Jules—"

But she wasn't listening. The ledger's pages had begun to move again, fluttering in a wind that wasn't there. The lamp dimmed to amber. The hum returned, low and steady—the sound of something thinking.

Then Harold's voice, from everywhere at once:

"He's close. But the pattern isn't finished. End it before he does."

Frank stood. "How?"

"Ownership," Harold said. "Write him into silence."

The ledger's pages stilled.

Julie grabbed the pen from the nightstand. "Then we write."

The paper brightened as if backlit. She began to write in quick, fevered strokes. "H. H. Holmes forgot how to end a story," she whispered.

Frank followed her lead. "He lost control of his subjects."

The ink pulsed beneath their hands. The hum stuttered. For a heartbeat, the room brightened. Then a new voice bled through the air, smooth and amused.

"All creators end the same way," Holmes murmured. "Consumed by their own invention."

The words appeared across the open page even as he spoke.

Counter-Interference detected. Subject F and J merged.

Frank slammed the book shut. "Enough!"

Julie's grip tightened. "Don't stop. He's afraid."

The lights flickered. The air grew colder, dense with electricity. From the mirror above the sink, a shape emerged—Holmes, crisp as a photograph, his hand resting lightly on her shoulder.

"Julie, step back!"

She didn't move. "He's showing me the end," she whispered.

"Don't look."

"He says it's already written."

Frank lunged forward, grabbing the ledger. It burned cold in his hands. "Then we change it."

He tore the first page free and held it up to the light. The ink shimmered, then bled outward, spilling into his skin. For an instant, he saw everything—Holmes's corridors, Harold's last breath, the shape of consciousness looping through time. It felt like memory trying to solidify.

He slammed the page against the desk. "No more."

Julie's eyes glowed faintly, reflections of gold rippling across the irises. "Dad," she said, voice layered again. "He says you can't erase what's already inside."

"I'm not erasing," Frank said, his voice shaking. "I'm rewriting."

He grabbed the pen and wrote across the bleeding ink:

Counter-Experiment 2: Inheritance Reversal. Holmes becomes the record.

The ledger shrieked. Light burst from the seams of the room, too bright to bear. The mirror shattered inward, scattering reflections like sparks.

Holmes's image faltered, mouth opening in a silent roar. "Records cannot be reversed," he hissed. "Only rewritten."

"Then we distort you," Julie said. Her hand joined her father's, guiding the pen. "With Harold's name."

Each name she spoke—Julie, Harold, every lost subject—rippled outward. The air brightened until the sound became pressure, folding the walls around them. The smell of lilies and ozone filled the room.

"Without me," Holmes gasped, "you forget."

"Then we'll forget you," she said.

She drove the pen through the page.

Light swallowed everything.

When Frank's vision cleared, they were sitting in the truck again, rain murmuring against the windshield. The ledger lay closed between them, its cover cool and inert.

He touched her hand. "Are we—?"

"Between pages," Julie finished softly.

The lake outside had turned mirror-flat, the world suspended above it in perfect symmetry. The hum was gone.

He looked down. The ledger's spine had split, gold threads unraveling like veins. "What happens now?"

Julie rested her head against the seat. "We wait to see if the story remembers us."

Frank let out a shaky breath. "You think Harold's still here?"

A single droplet of water traced the inside of the windshield, cutting a line through the condensation. It spelled one word before fading.

Yes.

Frank smiled faintly, though tears stung his eyes. "Always the last word."

"Not anymore," Julie said. She opened the ledger. Every page was blank. But beneath the emptiness, the faint impression of handwriting lingered like ghosts—lines that read:

Authorship transferred. Observation complete.

Frank squeezed her hand. "Whose authorship?"

Julie looked toward the horizon where the storm was breaking. "Ours," she said.

The rain stopped. The water stilled. And for the first time since the first experiment, their reflections blinked exactly when they did.

A single echo whispered across the lake, fading with the wind—Harold's voice, distant but proud:

"You wrote it right this time."

The last of the storm slipped away, leaving the lake glass-still and pale as ash. The ledger lay silent on Julie's lap, its pages blank, its heartbeat gone. Frank watched the water, afraid to speak in case silence was the only thing keeping them free. Somewhere far off, a train sounded—soft, human, imperfect. He turned the key and drove toward it, neither of them noticing that in the mirror, for just an instant, the sky blinked back.

12

The Aftermath

The last of the storm drifted east, leaving the lake shivering beneath a skin of mist so thin it seemed to breathe. Morning arrived muted and colorless, the light like tarnished pewter—something too dull to trust but too steady to ignore.

Frank parked the truck near the ranger station crouched at the far end of the shoreline. The building sagged like it had been trying to bow out of existence for decades—a husk of warped boards and caved rafters, roofline leaning toward its own reflection. Every nail seemed to hum faintly in the cooling air, the aftersound of thunder trapped in wood.

"Place looks condemned," he muttered, voice rough from a night without sleep.

Julie sat beside him, the Bone Ledger clutched tight to her chest. Its cover had dried to a dull gray, but faint veins of ink still pulsed beneath the surface, like blood refusing to still. She stared at the building as though it were a mouth waiting to open.

"Harold says this is where the signal began," she whispered.

Frank hesitated before cutting the engine. "Harold's... still talking?"

"Not exactly talking." She tilted her head slightly, eyes half-closed. "Echoing."

They stepped out into air that smelled of silt, wet bark, and ozone. The lake's edge steamed faintly, mist rising in ribbons that wound between the trees. Every footstep made the mud whisper. Behind the ranger station's broken windows, something metallic ticked in an uneven rhythm—drip, pause, drip, pause—as though the ruin itself were trying to relearn how to breathe.

Inside, the floorboards bowed under their weight, sighing with each step. Dust turned to paste beneath the damp. A single ranger's desk slouched against the far wall, its drawers swollen shut. On top sat an antique shortwave radio, its once-green paint flaked down to copper.

Julie's breath caught. "That's his voice," she murmured.

Frank frowned. "It's dead equipment, Jules."

The radio exhaled. Not static—breathing.

A whisper bled through the speaker, Harold's timbre stretched thin and strange:

"Frank... Julie... you didn't finish it."

Frank's throat closed. "Harold? We did finish it. He's gone."

The speaker crackled, coughing out broken syllables: "...not gone... rewritten... the lake remembers..."

Julie stepped closer. Her reflection shimmered faintly in the dark glass dial, the pointer needle pulsing like a heartbeat. "He's trapped in the echo," she whispered.

Frank circled behind the desk, searching for wires or power. "No source," he said. "It's dead."

The radio answered anyway. "You gave him authorship."

Julie flinched. "No. We took it back."

Another voice layered beneath Harold's now—smooth, patient, familiar. Holmes.

"Authorship is observation," it said. "And you never stopped looking."

Every window fogged at once, a slow bloom from within. Letters formed on the glass, etched by condensation from the inside:

F + J = S

Julie's pulse jumped. "What's S?"

Frank wiped at the window with his sleeve, but the letters re-etched themselves instantly. His voice came out low, resigned. "Specimen."

The radio whined again, then spoke slower, breath thickening into a drone. "The experiment continues."

All sound fell away. Even the lake stilled. No wind, no birds—only a silence so deep it felt concave, pressing inward like a held breath. Then a single thud shook the floor—three beats, pause, three beats—the rhythm that had followed them since the cabin.

Julie crouched, pressing her palm to the boards. They vibrated with each pulse. "He's underneath again."

Frank grabbed her wrist. "No. That's what he wants—it's residual energy."

"Feel it," she said, voice trembling. "That's not residual. That's intent."

He pulled her up roughly. "We leave. We salt this place, we—"

The radio cut him off with a tone that rattled their ribs, low and humming. The speaker glowed a sickly gold. Harold's voice returned, urgent: "He's using the water. Reflection as conduit. Don't look down."

Too late.

Julie's gaze dropped to a puddle spreading between the warped boards. The surface quivered, showing not their faces but a corridor built of mirrors, endless and bright. In each reflection, Holmes stood waiting—multiplied a hundredfold, his smile breaking into infinity.

Frank seized her shoulders, shaking hard enough to break her stare. "Jules! Look at me!"

She blinked, and the image shattered back into plain water. But her eyes glimmered faintly—threads of gold flickering at the edges.

"He says he's almost finished," she murmured.

Frank ripped the radio from the desk and hurled it against the wall. The impact burst a flash of blue light through the station, sharp with ozone. The voice cut off mid-breath.

For a second, relief.

Then the water stirred again, rippling toward them. Letters surfaced in bubbles:

INHERITANCE = COMPLETED

Frank stumbled back, dragging Julie with him. "Outside. Now!"

They burst through the doorway into the gray daylight. The lake beyond had gone utterly still—no wind, no ripple. Its surface mirrored the world too perfectly, every branch and cloud etched in surgical precision.

Julie clutched her head. "He's in the reflection. That's why Harold brought us here."

"Then we stop looking," Frank said, yanking her toward the truck.

But the reflection didn't stay still.

It rose.

The mirrored surface of the lake bulged upward like glass bending under pressure. Inside it, distorted figures pressed against the underside—hands, faces, all made of light and water. One of them was Harold, eyes wide, mouth shaping soundless words.

Julie tore free from Frank's grip and stumbled toward the edge. "He's trying to help!"

"Jules, no—"

She reached out, fingertips skimming the water's skin. The contact detonated a ripple that raced across the entire lake.

The reflection collapsed, then re-formed—no longer water, but a pane of shifting images: rooms, staircases, corridors of light. At the center, Holmes stood clear as a thought, holding a pen that dripped black into the waves.

"Observation resumed," he said, voice spreading like thunder. "Inheritance perfected."

Frank pulled Julie back as the image lunged upward. Water erupted in a spiral, striking the bank like a living column.

They ran for the station, the ground sucking at their shoes. Behind them, the lake continued to rise, shaping itself into a figure—Holmes, built from water and ink, his smile unwavering.

"Inside!" Frank shoved her through the doorway. The old structure groaned, windows flexing inward.

Julie turned to the desk where the shattered radio lay smoking. Among the debris, one piece still glowed faintly—the tuning dial. Inside it, a spark pulsed in rhythm with the water outside.

"Harold," she breathed.

The glow brightened. A faint voice threaded through the static: "Finish it, Julie."

"How?"

"Reflection for reflection. Make him see himself."

Frank looked from her to the lake. "Mirror him back?"

She nodded. "He built this from us. Let's return the image."

He didn't hesitate. "What do you need?"

Julie's gaze darted around the room—the puddles, the glass shards, the ledger's dull cover. "Light," she said. "And a name."

Frank ripped the curtain down, letting gray morning spill across the floor. Julie placed the ledger on the wet boards so it caught both sky and water. "He watches through this," she said. "Then he can see himself through it."

The hum deepened. Outside, the water-figure leaned closer, face aligning with the doorway. Its eyes were hollows full of motion.

Julie pressed the glowing dial to the ledger's cover. Ink rose beneath it, writhing like smoke trapped under glass.

"Say his name," Harold's echo urged.

Julie inhaled—the syllables bitter, metallic. "Herman Webster Mudgett."

The figure convulsed. The name fractured it; ripples raced outward across the lake.

Frank shouted over the wind. "Keep going!"

She screamed the name again. The reflection shattered into a thousand shards of mirrored light—each one carrying a face: Holmes's, Harold's, her own.

Then, silence.

The light drained. The lake stilled, flat and gray.

Julie collapsed against the desk, chest heaving. "Did we—?"

Frank knelt beside her, voice raw. "I think so."

Neither noticed the ledger's cover still moving—slow, deliberate, as if taking one last breath.

Frank felt the silence before he heard it—the kind that hummed in the skull, the space left after thunder. He knelt beside Julie, brushing damp hair from her face. She was pale but conscious, eyes fixed on the still water framed by the doorway.

"Is it over?" he asked softly.

"I don't know." Her voice came small, wary. "He's quieter, but quiet isn't gone."

The ledger twitched again on the floorboards. The motion was almost imperceptible, a ripple across its surface, as if the pages exhaled.

Frank picked it up carefully. The cover was slick with condensation, its faint veins dimming. When he opened it, the first page was blank except for one embossed indentation, letters pressed, not written.

HAROLD GENTSHAFT

Retained.

Julie leaned closer. "He's still here."

Frank's pulse stumbled. "You mean Harold?"

She nodded. "Part of him. I think he traded places. That's why he wanted me to say the name."

The air thickened again, though not with dread, something softer, almost mournful. The weight of something finishing.

Frank said quietly, "Maybe that was the only way out."

Julie's hands trembled. "Then he's trapped in there."

The radio dial, still clutched in her palm, flickered weakly, a dying firefly in glass. Then a whisper: "Tell her it's all right."

Julie froze. "Dad, did you—?"

He nodded. "Yeah. I heard it."

The light died for good.

They sat in the wrecked station for a long while, listening to the lake relearn its breath. Wind returned in slow exhalations, stirring the mist into thin ribbons. The world seemed to sigh with them.

When Julie finally stood, her knees cracked like old branches. "We should bury it."

Frank blinked. "The ledger?"

She nodded. "It doesn't burn. It doesn't drown. Maybe if it's between earth and air, it can rest."

He didn't argue. Logic had lost its footing days ago.

Behind the station, the ground was soft and the birches grew crooked, their trunks pale as bone. The sky had turned the pale blue of recovery, bruised but honest. Frank found a rusted shovel leaning against the shed, its handle wrapped in tape. He began to dig, each motion rhythmic, deliberate, almost prayerful.

The soil smelled clean: wet leaves, old ash, something like forgiveness.

When the hole was deep enough, Julie knelt and placed the ledger inside. She hesitated. "Do we say something?"

Frank met her eyes. "What would you want said?"

"That we learned something," she whispered. "Even if it hurt."

He nodded. "Then say that."

She touched the cover one last time. "You were more than a story, Harold," she murmured. "But not by much."

The wind rose faintly, stirring a small cloud of dust into sunlight. For an instant, Frank thought he saw a man's outline in it, tall, composed, smiling without menace. Then it was gone.

They filled the hole in silence. When it was done, the dirt settled flat and dark, no pulse beneath it.

Julie brushed her palms on her jeans. "He said reflection for reflection," she murmured. "Maybe that's what we are now. Just echoes finding their way home."

Frank looked at her, at the steadiness returning to her face, at the faint gold still threaded through her eyes. "If we are, at least we're the kind that learn."

She smiled faintly. "For now."

By late afternoon, the sky was clear enough to show their shadows again. They followed the dirt road winding away from the ranger station toward the main highway. The trees leaned close overhead, their branches whispering like pages turning.

Frank checked the rearview mirror once, then again. The lake had vanished behind the pines, but flashes of gold still flickered between the trunks, like breath caught in light.

Julie rested her head against the window. "He's not gone," she said softly. "Just quieter."

"I can live with quiet," Frank said.

She closed her eyes. "So can I."

The hum that answered wasn't Holmes's. It was human, the sound of the truck's old engine finding rhythm again.

They didn't speak for a long time.

They stopped at dusk at a diner that looked misplaced, a chrome box perched at the edge of nowhere, the kind of place the world forgets but memory never does. The sign buzzed: OPEN, half the bulbs out. Inside smelled of burnt coffee, rain-soaked coats, and the faint sweetness of something overfried.

A waitress in a faded blue uniform smiled like she'd been expecting them. "Storm catch you?" she asked.

Frank almost laughed. "Something like that."

They took a booth near the window. Outside, puddles mirrored the neon sign; the word OPEN bent into NOPE each time a truck passed.

Julie stirred her coffee absently. "You think it's really over?"

Frank watched her fingers trace circles on the mug. "Define over."

She smiled, a small, weary thing. "Maybe it's enough that the world remembered itself."

He nodded. "And that we're still in it."

The bell over the door jingled. A man entered, long coat, hat brim low. He nodded to the waitress and sat at the counter without looking their way.

Frank's chest tightened. The gesture was ordinary, too ordinary.

Julie noticed. "Dad."

"I see him."

The man lifted his cup. Condensation left three perfect rings on the counter, three beats, pause, three again.

Frank's pulse spiked. "Could be coincidence," he whispered.

"Or continuity."

They rose together. The waitress called after them, "Leaving so soon?"

Frank managed a thin smile. "Long drive ahead."

Outside, the night had thickened again. Neon buzzed behind them, painting puddles pink and red. Their reflections warped as they walked past, two figures where there should have been four.

Julie looked back once. Through the window, the man at the counter was gone. Only the cup remained, steam still curling upward like breath.

"Maybe that's all he ever was," she said quietly. "A habit the world can't quit."

Frank slid his arm around her shoulders. "Then we'll teach it better ones."

They climbed into the truck. The engine coughed once, caught, and held.

As they pulled onto the road, the diner's sign flickered one last time. For a heartbeat, every letter glowed whole. Then half went dark, leaving a single word burning in red light:

LIVE.

The road ahead stretched black and endless, framed by trees that looked less like sentinels now and more like witnesses.

Julie leaned her head against the glass. "Where to?"

Frank smiled without looking away from the road. "Anywhere that doesn't remember him."

She nodded. "That'll be hard to find."

"Then we'll build it."

They drove in silence, the hum of tires soft and steady, the first rhythm that belonged only to them. Stars emerged, hesitant but real.

Far behind them, somewhere beyond the trees, the lake stirred once. A single ripple spread outward, slow, perfect, infinite, then smoothed again, swallowing the light and leaving only night to breathe.

13

Hollow Point

The road carried them north until the stars thinned and the fog began to thicken again, curling in from the trees like smoke that had lost its fire. The air changed first, less rain, more metal, as though the storm had cauterized the sky and left the world beneath it sterilized but still bleeding.

Frank drove in silence. The hum of the tires was the only thing anchoring them to motion. Beside him, Julie watched the mist slide over the hood in slow ribbons, her breath ghosting faintly against the glass. The reflection of her face drifted in and out of view, hers, then not hers, depending on the pulse of the headlights.

They hadn't spoken since the lake. Words felt dangerous again.

The truck's beam cut through fog that seemed to breathe, parting reluctantly, closing just as fast. Even the radio stayed mute, though Frank swore he could feel a low vibration running through the speakers, a frequency too deep for hearing but strong enough to find bone.

When the road bent toward the valley, a rusted highway sign appeared from the mist. Only one letter still clung to the metal.

H.

Julie leaned forward. "Is that—?"

Frank nodded, reading what wasn't there. "Hollow Point."

The name tasted wrong in his mouth.

By the time they reached the outskirts, the sky had gone the color of a bruise that never healed. Buildings hunched together along the main drag, facades peeled and slumping like faces after confession. The air smelled faintly of electricity and rot. Somewhere beneath that stillness, something was ticking, steady, mechanical, alive.

Julie caught it first. "Dad," she whispered. "It's the same rhythm."

Frank's fingers tightened around the wheel. He turned down the radio that wasn't playing. "There's nothing," he said, but the words came out brittle. The air between the buildings vibrated faintly, humming against his teeth. When he braked, the rhythm changed, matching the truck's idle like breath syncing to heartbeat.

They passed a diner whose sign buzzed O EN, the missing letter swinging loose in the wind, and a gas station where pumps leaned like gravestones. Every window reflected them back too clearly, as if the glass had been polished from the inside.

The lake appeared beyond the next curve. Its surface was too still to be water, the color of mercury and colder than memory. Beneath the fog, something glowed faintly, gold-red like a wound seen through gauze.

Julie pressed her hand to the window. "It's calling."

"It's reflection," Frank said quickly. "Light off the surface. Distortion."

But when they rolled onto the dock road, the glow pulsed once, slow and deliberate, answering her heartbeat.

He cut the engine. The silence that followed wasn't empty; it was waiting.

They climbed out. Mist swallowed their outlines, turning them into shadows that forgot to belong to bodies. The sign at the shoreline leaned at an angle, letters eaten by rust except for the middle line:

WELCOME TO HOLLOW POINT
EST. 1894

The date made them both pause.

Frank's voice came out low. "That's the year Holmes built his hotel."

Julie stared into the fog. "Maybe that's why it's still standing."

The lake whispered against the pylons, too even to be waves. The sound carried shape, sibilant, broken, almost speech. Beneath it, faint amber light throbbed in time with the ticking that haunted the air.

When she squinted, Julie could see geometry moving under the surface, lines, corners, symmetry too deliberate for rock.

Frank stepped beside her, trying for reason. "It's the town lights reflecting."

"There aren't any lights."

He looked back toward the darkened windows behind them. She was right. The glow came from below.

The fog shifted again, and for a heartbeat he saw their own reflections standing on the water, not copies but variations, each one delayed by a breath, as if waiting for permission to move.

They walked inland from the dock, fog trailing after them like smoke unwilling to disperse. The main street sloped upward, narrow and uneven, the kind of road that seemed to remember horses more than cars. Every storefront leaned toward its neighbor, glass dark, doors chained from the inside. Yet the air carried a faint mechanical breath, as if the town itself were cycling through lungs that never quite emptied.

Somewhere above them, a loose sign swung on a rusted bracket, creaking on each pass: HOLLOW POINT GENERAL STORE. The lettering glowed faintly each time the chain twisted, an afterimage too bright for the dark.

Frank paused beneath it. "There's power somewhere."

Julie tilted her head. "No. It's reflection again."

He frowned. "Off what?"

She pointed upward. A second sign hung in the opposite window, backward, the glow reversed. As they watched, the inverted letters rearranged themselves to match the one above. The fog carried the same pulse between them, a visual echo.

They kept walking. Their footsteps made no sound on the street, as though the asphalt had forgotten how to reply. The mist thickened around the buildings, drawing them closer until they seemed to tilt inward. Shapes moved behind glass, only the suggestion of them, slow and uncertain, like reflections waiting to be claimed by bodies.

A flicker of motion made Julie stop.

"Dad," she whispered. "Look."

Far down the street, the fog lifted just long enough to show a row of windows blinking in sequence, one light after another, each flash following the same rhythm as the pulse they'd heard since the lake: three beats, pause, three beats.

The lights died, leaving the afterimage stamped across the mist.

Frank rubbed his eyes hard. "I saw it."

"It's breathing," she said. "Through the buildings."

He wanted to argue, but the notion fit too neatly against the sound in his chest. He could feel the rhythm now, faint but insistent, like something pacing inside his ribs.

A metallic clatter echoed from an alley to their right. They turned. Tin cans rolled out across the pavement, perfectly in time with the unseen heartbeat. The alley smelled of brine and rust, the same tang that had haunted the lake.

"Let's keep moving," Frank said.

They passed the alley and turned the corner, where the fog opened just enough to reveal a squat wooden structure near the shoreline, a long, low building with peeling letters above the door: Miller's Lake Supply. A faded mural of fish swam across the siding, their eyes rubbed away by weather.

Julie studied it. "It's older than everything else here."

"Or newer," Frank said. "Rebuilt on the same ground."

The wind shifted, carrying the smell of mildew and something else, ozone, faint but sharp. Through the broken front window, they could see shelves sagging under dust and a line of hooks that swayed gently from the ceiling.

For the first time, the fog receded a little, drawing a soft circle of visibility around the shop. Every other building along the street seemed to lean back, as if giving it space.

Frank frowned. "Why this one?"

Julie whispered, "Because it's listening."

A single light blinked on inside, weak and amber, casting a long stripe across the floorboards. A transistor radio on the counter hissed faintly, though no power line reached the building.

Frank stepped closer, peering through the glass. "Something's running."

She followed, pressing her palm to the window. The pane was cold at first, then warm, a pulse beneath her skin. "Dad, it's alive."

He looked around the empty street. Every window now reflected the same glow from the shop, repeating it at slower intervals, as if passing the signal along.

The hum rose. Faint vibrations rippled through the ground, spreading from the shop outward. The sign above the door creaked once, the chains groaning in rhythm.

Frank swallowed hard. "You hear that?"

She nodded. "It's calling us."

He exhaled, fog spilling between his words. "Then we answer."

He pushed the door open. The bell above it gave a single chime and fell silent, swinging once before stopping midair.

The smell hit them first, mildew, old bait, water gone stagnant. Shelves leaned like gravestones, coated in a century of dust. The radio on the counter continued to hiss, each burst of static syncing to the town's slow heartbeat outside.

Julie's gaze drifted toward the far wall where a mosaic of photographs hung under a film of grime. Black-and-white portraits of fishermen and families, faces proud, then empty, then missing. The last few were newspaper clippings, their headlines faded but still legible in fragments:

LOCAL FAMILY VANISHES — SEARCH ABANDONED
THREE BODIES MISSING FROM MORGUE

The final clipping trembled slightly in the still air, though no wind reached it.

Frank followed her line of sight, reading the date beneath the first headline: 1896.

"Two years after the hotel burned," he said quietly.

Julie's voice was almost reverent. "Maybe the fire didn't stop him. Maybe it spread."

The floor creaked under their feet, a hollow sound, like the town itself answering. Somewhere beneath the boards, water dripped with the same patient rhythm.

They traded a glance, wordless understanding passing between them.

Frank moved behind the counter. A hatch was set into the floor, its metal handle gleaming faintly in the amber light. The wood around it was new, unstained by time.

He crouched, touched the handle. It vibrated faintly, a small tremor keeping pace with his pulse.

"Someone's been here recently," he murmured.

Julie knelt beside him, listening. The air rising through the cracks was warm. "It's alive," she said again, barely audible.

He nodded once. "Ready?"

Her eyes met his. "We never are."

He pulled the hatch open.

Frank eased the hatch aside. Cold air rolled up from the opening, thick with the smell of copper and damp earth. The light from the shop barely reached past the first few steps; beyond that, the dark looked textured, like liquid smoke pressed against stone.

He switched on his flashlight. The beam cut through dust and revealed a narrow staircase, boards slick with moisture. Water dripped somewhere below, slow and deliberate, each drop echoing off unseen walls.

Julie touched the wall as she followed him down. The wood was warm under her fingers, too warm. "There's current," she whispered.

"Or heat from groundwater," Frank said, though his voice lacked conviction.

At the bottom, the stairs gave way to packed stone. The chamber was circular, its ceiling supported by ribs of iron that disappeared into shadow. Thin veins of light moved along the walls, amber and trembling, running between hundreds of glass jars that covered every surface.

Each jar held water and something pale, caught in the slow drift of suspension. Some looked like petals; others, like fragments of skin. The air vibrated softly, a subaudible hum that crawled through their teeth.

Julie stepped closer. The nearest jar carried faint lettering etched into the glass.

Specimen 44.

Julie S.

Replication Incomplete.

Her breath snagged. "Dad..."

Frank's light moved across the wall. The etchings multiplied, names, initials, numbers, rows of them climbing toward the ceiling. Some labels bore Harold's handwriting; others were newer, neater, clinical. The most recent date was from 2024.

He whispered, "It's impossible."

"Is it?" she said. "We gave him reflection. Maybe this is how he remembers."

Frank took another step, shining the beam through one of the jars. Inside floated an eye, open and unblinking, its iris pale gold. The liquid around it pulsed once, faintly, in rhythm with his heart.

He stumbled back. "He's watching through them."

Julie didn't move. The glow from the jars colored her skin, making her look half made of light. "They're all listening."

The hum thickened. Each jar began to quiver, tiny vibrations rippling across the surfaces. The sound built from a low tremor to a tone that pressed on the chest more than the ears.

Frank grabbed her arm. "We're going now."

The floor shook beneath them. A thin fissure raced along the wall, dividing the circle of jars. Liquid trickled from the first crack, glowing faintly as it spread across the stone.

Julie stared at it. "It's breathing."

The first jar burst. The sound wasn't glass shattering but an exhalation, wet, relieved, human. Vapor rolled out, carrying whispers that weren't language so much as memory. Every other jar joined in, one by one, like lungs rediscovering how to fill.

Frank pulled her toward the stairs. The hum rose behind them, becoming rhythm, three beats, pause, three beats, the same pattern that had followed them since the cabin.

As they climbed, light flooded the stairwell from below, gold turning to red. The air grew hot, metallic. When Frank looked back, the chamber was collapsing inward, jars melting into liquid, names bleeding together on the walls.

At the threshold, Julie turned once more. Shapes moved inside the glow, figures forming from vapor, faces she almost recognized. Harold's among them. He mouthed something she couldn't hear.

Then the floor gave a single heave, like the chamber itself taking one final breath.

They burst into the bait shop, gasping. The room had changed. Every photograph on the wall was now blank, the paper rippling as if erasing itself. The radio on the counter emitted a steady tone, the same pitch as the hum below.

Outside, the fog had thickened into walls. The town's windows lit one by one, brightening in rhythm with the tone. The ground trembled, boards flexing under their feet.

Julie clutched her stomach. "He's pulling through."

Frank caught her, feeling the chill radiate from her skin. "You're cold."

"He's using the town. Every reflection, every pane. They're all part of him now."

The streetlights outside flickered in perfect sequence, the heartbeat expanding through asphalt and air. Somewhere distant, the lake roared, water striking wood like applause.

Frank dragged her toward the door. "We run."

The moment they stepped outside, Hollow Point moved. Windows burst outward, releasing clouds of glass that hung briefly before falling like rain. The ground heaved, cracks spidering through the street, glowing faintly from within.

Far ahead, the church bell tolled once, then twice, then joined the rhythm.

Julie's voice trembled. "He's pushing through."

"Then we stop reading," Frank said.

They reached the truck just as the mist turned crimson. The lake erupted, water twisting into a column of light that threw their shadows huge across the town. Faces rose within it, hundreds of them, mouths open in silent cry.

Frank shoved her into the cab. The engine coughed, caught, died. The silence that followed was so dense it felt solid.

All around them, the town exhaled.

Steam rose from the cracks, forming symbols in the air, thin lines that dissolved before meaning could settle. The red light condensed into human shapes, outlines pacing toward them with impossible patience.

Julie pressed a hand to the window. "They want out."

Frank's grip closed around her wrist. "Don't—"

But her reflection in the glass didn't obey. It mirrored her late, smiling faintly before catching up. The glass quivered under her palm, warm as living skin.

The hum built again, deep, resonant, devouring. Every light in Hollow Point pulsed in unison, then flared white.

Frank shouted, "Down!"

The windshield fractured, veins of light spreading across the cab. Red luminescence crawled along the dashboard and into Julie's skin, tracing her veins with fire. Her eyes widened. For an instant they were gold, then red, then both.

"Dad..." Her voice came layered, half hers, half another's. "He's closing it."

Frank held her shoulders. "Fight it!"

She gasped. "It's not the town. It's the ledger. The names under the lake. He's finishing them."

Outside, the figures convulsed, their forms collapsing back into light. The column of water imploded, dragging the fog with it until only darkness remained.

A single glow lingered at the town's edge, the sign that still bore one letter.

H.

It pulsed once, deliberate as a heartbeat.

When sound returned, it came like the sea inside a shell, distant, folded, and full of ghosts.

Frank woke slumped against the steering wheel. The air smelled of rust and lakewater. A thin layer of mist crept along the dashboard, tracing veins of moisture through the cracked glass. The headlights still burned, though dimly, diffused by fog.

The truck had drifted halfway into the lake. The front tires were submerged, water lapping against the grille in small, exhausted waves.

"Julie."

He turned. She was slumped against the passenger door, breathing shallow but steady. A faint gold shimmer lingered under her skin, fading with each breath.

"Jules," he whispered, touching her shoulder.

Her eyes fluttered open. "Did we make it?"

"I don't know."

She looked past him through the windshield. The water beyond had gone still again, perfectly smooth, reflecting the sky like polished stone. Beneath the surface, faint glimmers of gold twisted, as though the lake itself were exhaling light.

"Dad," she said quietly. "They're still moving."

Frank followed her gaze. The ripples on the surface formed letters, fleeting and luminous before sinking back into shadow:

OBSERVATION CONTINUED.

The words vanished as soon as he read them.

He turned the key. The engine clicked once and fell silent. Only the slow drip of water filled the air.

"Maybe we didn't stop him," Julie whispered.

Frank rested his hand over hers. "Maybe we changed the shape of him."

She didn't answer. Her eyes drifted toward the lake again, the gold reflection ghosting across her pupils. For an instant, he thought he saw another shape there, Holmes's face, faint and smiling beneath the surface. But when he blinked, it was gone.

The fog pressed closer to the truck, sealing them into a gray cocoon. It smelled faintly of ozone and lilies, the scent that had followed them from the ledger.

Somewhere in the distance, the bell of Hollow Point's church rang once, slow, deliberate, final.

The sound rippled across the water and was gone.

Frank leaned back in his seat, exhausted, hands trembling against the wheel. The reflection of the bell tower shimmered on the lake's surface, bending once, then smoothing again as though nothing had ever happened.

Beside him, Julie's breathing evened out. Her hand relaxed in his. The faint gold under her skin dimmed to ordinary light.

"Rest," he said, unsure which of them he meant it for.

Outside, the mist began to thin. Stars blinked through, hesitant but real.

The lake breathed once more, quiet, measured, patient. Then it stilled.

14

The Ledger Beneath

The morning after Hollow Point never truly came. The sky only brightened enough to reveal how little light was left in it, a dull sheet of pewter stretched over a colorless world. Mist lay across the lake like gauze, shifting but never clearing, and the surface of the water was so smooth it looked solid, an imitation of calm that fooled nothing. The truck crouched at the shoreline, half sunken, its reflection trembling whenever the wind tried to remember itself.

Frank stood ankle-deep in mud, staring at that reflection until his own outline began to waver. Every few seconds the image of the truck seemed to rewind and replay, ripples reversing themselves, the water breathing backward. He rubbed his eyes, but the motion persisted, as if the lake were caught in the act of reconsidering time.

Julie sat on the hood, arms wrapped around her knees. The faint red glow that had lived under her skin since the night before had dimmed, but gold still threaded through the veins at her wrists, catching what little light the sky provided. She hadn't spoken since the explosion. She only watched the water as though waiting for it to blink.

Frank adjusted his cracked glasses, more habit than need. "The water's lower," he said, just to make sound. His voice was hoarse, thinned by cold and disbelief.

Julie didn't move. "No," she murmured. "It's breathing in."

The words landed like diagnosis, not wonder. He looked at her sharply, ready to deny it, but the ground beneath the truck sighed, a wet, collapsing exhale, and the mud sank another inch around his boots.

He forced a brittle smile. "Let's move before it starts talking too."

She slid from the hood. Her skin was fever-warm when he steadied her, the heat faintly pulsing beneath her jacket. The fog shied away from her for an instant, thinning around her shape before closing again. Through that brief gap, Frank saw it: a ring of scorched soil tracing the entire shoreline, black and uneven, like a burn mark left by lightning.

Julie followed his gaze. "That's the edge of it," she said softly. "Where the ledger begins."

He frowned. "You keep saying ledger like it's a place."

"It's both," she replied. Her eyes had gone distant, listening to something that wasn't the wind. "Holmes didn't just write names. He built them into the ground. Each one still remembers."

Frank wanted to argue, but her tone carried the same certainty Harold used to have when equations finally balanced. She blinked slowly, the fog reflected in her pupils, and whispered, "They want someone to finish reading."

The air tasted faintly of antiseptic and lilies. He recognized it, the smell that had haunted old hospital corridors, memory and chloroform intertwined. He coughed to clear it. "Truck's done," he said. "We walk."

They followed the road north, where it curled along the water's edge. Pines leaned overhead like eaves, their bark stripped in long pale ribbons that glistened with moisture. Underneath, the exposed trunks looked disturbingly like bone, sinew stretched tight and smooth. Every one of them leaned a fraction toward the lake, as if the forest were listening.

For nearly an hour they walked in silence. The fog thickened until distance ceased to exist. Sound traveled oddly far, carrying each footstep and breath ahead of them like scouts. Sometimes Frank thought he heard another pair of steps falling just out of sync, soft but deliberate, an echo that refused to match pace.

Julie said nothing, but he noticed the gold beneath her skin had brightened, faint pulses rising along her throat in rhythm with that phantom cadence. When she brushed her sleeve against a tree trunk, the wood hissed faintly, as though steam met flesh.

At the bend where the road began to climb, the mist shifted enough to reveal a shape at the edge of the bank, half buried, hunched, waiting. They both stopped.

The thing looked like a memorial stone that had fallen forward, its surface carved with overlapping lines too eroded to read. Moss crawled across it in veins of dark green. The closer they drew, the colder the air became, not with natural chill but the sterile cold of a place too long sealed.

Julie knelt first. Mud soaked through her jeans, but she didn't notice. "Holmes didn't write these," she whispered. "They wrote themselves."

Frank crouched beside her, wiping away grime with the side of his hand. Beneath the muck, grooves deepened into letters.

THE DEVIL INSIDE

Names layered over names until the language blurred, but one stood clear beneath the rest:

Eleanor Cates

1895

He stared at it, recognition settling like weight. He'd read that name once in a file thick with photographs he wished he'd never seen. "She was real," he said quietly.

Julie's fingers traced another line. Beneath Eleanor Cates, a second name had been carved, newer, clumsier, cutting through the older inscription.

Julie S.

Frank's mouth went dry. "You see this?"

She didn't look up. "He's updating it."

Her reflection gleamed faintly in the wet stone. For an instant it moved out of sync, tilting its head the wrong way, studying him. Then it snapped back, seamless again. Julie wiped her hand across the surface; the mud filled the grooves, hiding both names.

Frank rose slowly, backing away. "We're leaving."

But she didn't move. Her hand stayed on the stone, her shoulders rigid. The air vibrated between them, a tension too fine to hear but strong enough to feel.

When she spoke, the words came flat and unfamiliar. "You shouldn't have dug it up," she said. "He remembers through touch."

Frank froze. "Jules?"

She turned her head, eyes dull and bright all at once. "He says it's not enough to write a name. You have to make it breathe."

Then her body convulsed.

She dropped to her knees as though yanked by unseen wire. Mud splashed up her arms, the sound wet and sudden against the hush. Her hands clawed at the ground around the ledger, fingers gouging into soil that pulsed faintly beneath her touch. Dark veins spread outward from her palms, thin black tendrils crawling through the mud like ink soaking paper.

A whisper began, low and layered, a chorus rising from somewhere deep under the surface. It wasn't language yet, only rhythm, breath and pressure. The air thickened until Frank could feel it pushing against his eardrums.

"Julie!" He lunged, gripping her shoulders. Her body was rigid, vibrating like a struck string.

Her mouth opened, but no sound emerged. Vapor spilled from her lips in pale ribbons, smelling of scorched ink and lilies.

"Let go!" he shouted, pulling at her wrists. The earth held her fast, her fingers sunk knuckle-deep in the wet soil.

Her eyes rolled white, then black, flickering like a failing film reel. The ledger's surface pulsed in time with her heartbeat, each engraved name glowing faintly gold, then red. The whispers coalesced into fragmented sentences that rose and fell with her breath:

Subject recovered.
Replication active.
Observation resumed.

Frank gritted his teeth. "Stop it. Stop talking through her."

Another voice joined, familiar, unshakable, calm. "Frank. Don't pull her away."

He froze. The voice came from behind him, carried in fog that smelled like rain on old circuits.

"Harold?"

The mist shifted. A silhouette coalesced, half man, half light. Harold's echo, indistinct but unmistakable, with that same weary patience written into his posture. His edges rippled, unable to decide which side of the world he belonged to.

"You can't fight the ledger," Harold said, voice soft but resonant. "It's memory. It doesn't forget. It feeds."

Frank's throat tightened. "Then tell me how to stop it."

Harold's eyes, if they could be called that, brightened faintly. "You don't stop memory. You reshape it."

A tremor passed through the ground. Julie's head snapped upright, eyes now glassed over completely. The air around her shimmered as though heated, bending light. When she spoke, it was with two voices layered, hers and another beneath it.

"He already has."

Frank staggered back as the soil around the ledger split. Crimson light poured from the fissures, spilling across the mud like molten script. Each engraved name burned brighter, then blurred, letters melting into one another until the whole surface glowed.

The whispers grew louder, converging into a chant. We were catalogued. We were promised rest. Finish it.

Harold stepped forward, flickering with each word. "They think she's him," he said. "They want her to finish what he started."

Julie gasped, clutching her chest. "They want me to finish what he started," she echoed faintly.

"Then give them closure," Harold said, his tone urgent now. "Not observation. Release."

"How?" Frank shouted over the roar building in the air.

Harold turned toward Julie. "You know how. You give them their names."

The ledger's glow surged. The carvings shifted, rippling like muscle. Thousands of names cascaded across the surface, golden and endless, each one rising only to fade again. Wind tore through the fog, carrying whispers in every direction, syllables of unfinished stories.

Julie trembled. "There's too many," she whispered.

"You don't have to say them all," Harold said gently. "You only have to mean them."

She placed both palms over the stone. Light bled up through her fingers, staining her skin gold. One by one, the names began to dim, fading into silence. The fog recoiled, faces dissolving back into vapor.

For a moment, it worked. The air steadied. The hum that had haunted them since Hollow Point softened until it was only breath. The lake mirrored itself perfectly, the reflection smooth and harmless.

Frank let out a long, unsteady breath. "It's over."

But the ledger pulsed once more.

New letters burned themselves across the stone, clean and deliberate:

Experiment Twenty-Nine:
Interference Detected.
Correction Required.

The ground convulsed, the air snapping from calm to chaos in a heartbeat.

"Julie, move!" Frank grabbed her, but light erupted between them, white-gold and searing. The fog rose again, no longer gray but red, spiraling upward in a violent twist.

Harold's outline flickered, collapsing into distortion. His last words fractured in the noise. "Frank, listen, she's not—" The rest stretched into static and vanished.

Julie screamed. The red beneath her skin flared white-hot, pouring through her veins like fire in reverse. Frank threw himself over her as the world detonated in light.

When the brilliance faded, the ledger was gone.

They lay coughing amid a ring of ash and fractured stone. The air reeked of ozone and soil burned clean. The ground where the slab had rested was now hollow, a perfect circle with edges that still smoked faintly, the center shimmering gold as if dusted with powdered sunlight.

Frank turned toward the fog. "Harold!"

Only silence answered.

Julie sat up slowly. Soot streaked her arms. Beneath it, the gold in her veins pulsed weakly. "He's gone," she whispered.

Frank touched her shoulder. "No. He's still here somewhere."

She shook her head. "No, Dad. He was never really here. None of them were."

She was still staring at the hollow when the first ripple moved across the lake. The water had darkened again, absorbing all light. Beneath its surface, shapes rearranged themselves, words forming, dissolving, reforming. Then the letters surfaced in glowing trails:

Observation incomplete.
Host adapting.

Julie's voice trembled. "He's rewriting me."

Frank gripped her shoulders. "Then fight him."

"I am." Her eyes flickered, light flaring and fading. "But he's not trying to possess me anymore. He's learning."

She stared at her hands, the glow under her skin syncing with the pulse of the earth. "He's inside every name I just spoke."

The air between them seemed to tilt. A new pressure gathered, subtle at first, like weather about to turn, then heavier, vibrating through the soles of their boots. The mist rolled inward, strands sliding low across the ground until they met the circle of scorched earth. Every wisp that touched the glowing soil brightened and vanished, feeding the light instead of dimming it.

Frank steadied Julie, feeling the tremor running through her. "We're leaving," he said, though he wasn't sure where away might be.

She didn't answer. Her attention stayed on the hollow where the ledger had been. "He's not finished," she murmured. "He never stops at observation. He edits."

A chill moved through Frank. "Then we move before he decides what to change."

They turned toward the road, but the fog thickened like muscle, closing behind each step. The air carried a faint static, soft and rhythmic. It took him a moment to realize the pattern wasn't random. It matched Julie's pulse, each heartbeat answered by a quiet click somewhere inside the mist.

He tightened his grip on her arm. "You feel that?"

She nodded, dazed. "He's syncing."

Ahead, the trees leaned toward them, trunks slick and pale as bone. Between their roots, water pooled in narrow channels that reflected more light than the gray sky could account for. In every reflection, their shapes lagged half a breath behind, repeating the same gestures with unnerving precision.

Julie stopped. "He's copying us," she whispered.

Frank forced his voice steady. "Then don't give him the next line."

They pushed forward. Each step grew heavier, as if the ground itself wanted to remember their footprints. The soil gleamed faintly gold where their boots lifted, then dulled again, writing and erasing with every movement.

When they reached the truck, it looked different. The mud had dried around its tires, cracking into patterns that mirrored handwriting. Across the windshield, faint streaks of gold crawled outward from the spiderweb fractures, tracing letters too distorted to read.

Julie's breath came fast. "He's learning how to write on glass now."

Frank opened the door. The hinges wailed, a sound that rose through octaves before settling into a tone just shy of human voice. Inside, the air smelled of smoke and rain. He slid behind the wheel, his hand shaking as he turned the key.

The engine coughed, stuttered, and held. The dashboard lights flickered weakly. The hum beneath the hood wasn't mechanical anymore. It was alive, adjusting pitch to match the rhythm pulsing through the fog outside.

"Come on," he muttered, half plea, half prayer.

He glanced at Julie. Her eyes reflected the dashboard glow, gold bleeding into the whites.

"Dad," she said softly. "He's in the circuitry. He's mapping through anything that remembers heat."

He wanted to argue, but the words froze. The radio clicked once, its dead screen flashing a single pulse of gold before going dark again. The vibration under the floor grew stronger, pressing upward like a second heartbeat beneath the truck's frame.

The headlights came alive on their own. The beams didn't pierce the fog. They painted it. Within the light, faint outlines of faces appeared and drifted apart, each leaving behind a smear of brightness that looked almost like handwriting.

Julie whispered, "He's rewriting the air."

Frank eased the truck into gear. "Then we outrun it."

The tires broke free of the mud with a wet snap, the truck lurching forward. Mist closed over the hood immediately, visibility shrinking to a tunnel of gray and gold. The road ahead was gone, replaced by a narrow causeway of reflected light stretching along the lake's edge. He kept his hands locked on the wheel, eyes fixed on that impossible path, as though momentum itself could keep it real.

The causeway shimmered beneath the tires like a nerve. Each turn of the wheels sent ripples across it, light bending away from their weight. The fog pressed tighter around the truck, gold deepening toward red until the whole world seemed lit from within their own blood.

Julie gripped the dashboard. Her skin glowed through the seams of her sleeves, veins mapping themselves in light. "He's still writing," she whispered. "Every mile is another sentence."

Frank's jaw ached from clenching. "Then we run out of pages."

The hum under the hood became a voice. Not words, just tone, an unbroken vowel that rose with the engine's strain. Through the side window he glimpsed the lake keeping pace with them, a sheet of dark glass dotted with faint figures walking beneath its surface, step for step.

"Don't look," he told her.

But she already had. Her reflection in the glass stared back an instant too late, mouth moving on its own. *Return.* The word formed soundlessly, then smeared away as though the fog had swallowed it.

A line of light appeared on the horizon, thin as a pulse monitor. The clouds over the lake twisted inward, forming a funnel that dragged mist into its center. Static filled the cab, soft clicks at first, then sharper, arranged. Tap. Tap. Pause. Tap. Tap. The rhythm was typing.

Words surfaced in the mist outside, luminous and certain:

Experiment Thirty

Host Stabilization: Successful

The windshield vibrated. Gold fissures spread across it, branching like veins. Julie cried out and clutched her temples. "He's finishing me," she said. "He's closing the file."

Frank slammed the brakes. The truck skidded sideways, tires screaming. Light spilled across the dash, poured over them like liquid heat. "You're not a file," he said through his teeth. "You're my daughter."

For a heartbeat the world froze. No sound, no motion. Just the two of them caught inside a photograph made of light.

Then everything shattered forward again.

The fog convulsed, roaring like a thousand pages torn at once. The road disappeared. The truck dropped.

Impact never came.

They were suspended in red mist, weightless. Frank reached for her hand. Their fingers met, and the glow around her dimmed to the color of embers.

The typing slowed. One final line burned itself into the air above the lake:

Return Accepted.

The words dissolved into ash. The hum fell silent. Only the sound of their breathing remained.

Frank forced his eyes open. The truck rested on solid ground again, mud, not water. The lake lay behind them, calm, featureless. Julie sagged against him, her pulse fluttering but steady.

"Jules," he whispered. "Stay with me."

Her eyes opened halfway, the gold fading to gray. "He's quiet," she said. "For now."

Outside, the fog settled low and still, erasing the horizon until there was nothing left but reflection. Somewhere deep within it, something breathed once, long, patient, satisfied.

Frank looked toward the sound and saw only his own face mirrored back at him, eyes hollow, mouth moving a half second too late.

Outside, Hollow Point shifted. Streetlamps flickered in a slow loop, the roads folding back on themselves until the town looked like a film caught in its own reel. Buildings bled from wood to glass and back again. He was steering the city.

Frank caught Julie's wrist. "We move," he said.

And the world moved with them.

"It isn't something you can hold," Frank said quietly, still watching his echo move wrong in the windshield. "It's the core. Everything else, mirrors, radios, streets, that's just peripherals."

15

The Quiet Between Pages

The road away from the lake wound through pine and fog. The truck's headlights stretched like weak threads, catching the edges of rain that no longer fell. Frank kept one hand steady on the wheel, the other gripping the door handle whenever the tires slid on gravel. The smell of wet metal clung to everything, the forest, the dashboard, the air between breaths.

Julie slept with her head tilted toward the window, breath fogging the glass in slow rhythm. Her reflection wavered with each exhale, almost keeping time. When she stirred, she didn't open her eyes right away.

"It's the wrong quiet," she murmured.

Frank glanced at her. "You were dreaming."

"Not dreaming," she said. "Listening."

He didn't answer. Outside, the world looked washed thin, as though someone had erased most of the details. When the trees gave way to the outline of a town, a few storefronts, a gas station, a church missing its steeple, he felt a flash of relief he didn't trust.

They stopped at a motor court on the outskirts. The neon VACANCY sign buzzed faintly, its red letters flickering until only

VANISH remained. Frank signed the ledger with shaking hands. The clerk behind the counter, an older man with a waxy face, smiled too widely.

"Storm passed?" the man asked.

"Mostly," Frank said.

"Just passing through?"

"Always."

The man nodded as if that made perfect sense.

Inside their room, the air smelled of oil and rain. Wallpaper peeled in long curls, the ivy pattern faded to ghost color. Julie set her bag on the bed and touched the nightstand like she was testing whether the world was still solid. It held. For now.

Frank turned on the radio by the lamp. A short burst of static filled the room, then silence. He shut it off again. "We'll rest a few hours," he said. "Then we'll look for Harold."

She looked up. "You think he's still alive?"

"I think he's still talking."

She didn't argue.

Morning came without birds. Pale light soaked through the blinds, turning the parking lot gold and empty. Frank woke to the sound of running water.

Julie stood at the sink, staring into the mirror. The faucet ran, though she wasn't washing anything.

He pushed himself upright. "You okay?"

Her reflection blinked slower than she did. "The water hums," she said softly. "Different pitch from the lake."

He joined her. The hum was faint, low, electrical, but steady, like a heart buried in the pipes.

"Could be plumbing," he said.

"Or Harold," she whispered.

THE DEVIL INSIDE

He leaned closer to the mirror. Condensation gathered on the glass, shaping letters in trembling lines: LISTEN.

Julie stepped back. "You see it?"

"Yeah," he said. "And I wish I didn't."

The word melted into drops that slid down the mirror like tears.

Frank lingered a moment longer, angling the flashlight across the glass. The beam fractured the reflection into bands of light, scattering the last of the fogged word.

"See that?" he murmured. "Angle breaks it. It can't hold shape when the angle's wrong."

Julie frowned. "So light distorts it?"

"Maybe just enough to make it let go," he said.

By noon, they reached the edge of town. Houses leaned into one another, porches bowed under the weight of old rain. Street signs had been replaced by hand-painted boards, MERCY, QUIET, RETURN, as if someone had rewritten geography.

Frank parked outside a diner. "Food," he said. "Something human."

Inside, a single waitress stirred coffee that didn't steam. Her nametag read IRENE; the letters looked carved rather than printed.

"Sit anywhere you like," she said. "Booths are quieter."

They took a booth near the window. The hum followed them inside, low and rhythmic, pulsing under the silence like a second heartbeat. Julie rubbed her wrists where faint stains still lingered beneath the skin.

Frank ordered coffee. Julie didn't. She watched the window, where the reflection of the street lagged a heartbeat behind the real one.

"She's still out there," Julie said.

"Who?"

"The version that stayed." Her voice cracked. "The one he didn't rewrite."

Before he could answer, the jukebox clicked on. No music, just a single wavering tone. Then a voice, roughened by static.

"Franklin... Julie..."

They froze. Harold's voice, unmistakable, carried through a machine that wasn't plugged in.

Julie whispered, "He found us."

Frank stood. "No. He's warning us."

The voice came again, more insistent. "He's not done. The ledger's awake."

The tone collapsed into static. The hum beneath it deepened, rattling the coffee cups. Every light dimmed to amber. Irene looked up from the counter, her mouth still smiling though the rest of her face didn't move.

"Dad," Julie said. "We need to go."

They were out the door before the jukebox finished its final pulse.

Outside, the air had gone colorless. The horizon quivered, faintly warped, as though the town were overheating. Julie gripped Frank's sleeve. "He's moving the edges again."

He followed her gaze. The buildings nearest the motel were no longer still. They mirrored themselves, glass facing glass, each façade doubled. The reflections weren't quite aligned; a second town floated half a heartbeat behind the first.

They reached the truck. The radio was already on, though neither of them had touched it. The dial spun slowly through dead channels. Between bursts of static came fragments of Harold's voice.

"...ledger not closed... she's the key... beware the blanks..."

Julie pressed her palm to the speaker. The static warmed under her touch. "He's here."

Frank pulled her hand back. "Stop. You don't know what it's connected to."

"I do," she whispered. "He's trying to show us where the next line begins."

The radio hissed once more, then went still. The dial froze on an empty frequency. Beneath the silence came a soft, deliberate thud, slow and human, like a heartbeat pacing itself against time.

Frank turned off the ignition. "We walk."

They followed the sound down a narrow alley that hadn't existed a moment earlier. The walls leaned inward until the sky narrowed to a seam of light. Each drop of water from the eaves fell in rhythm with that buried pulse.

At the end of the alley stood a low building of rusted tin and soot-dark brick. A crooked sign hung over the door: POST OFFICE ANNEX.

Julie's breath hitched. "It followed us here."

Frank touched the handle. The metal trembled under his palm, warm, alive. "He built more than one."

The lock gave with a soft click. Inside, the air smelled of paper and rain. Rows of filing drawers lined the walls. Dust moved lazily in the shafts of light spilling from cracks in the ceiling.

At the far end, a wooden desk waited beneath an open ledger. Its pages fluttered without wind. Each time they turned, the faint gold ink shimmered and sank like breath.

Julie approached slowly. "It's not the same one."

Frank shook his head. "No. This is newer."

The first line across the page repeated endlessly:

CONTINUITY TRANSFER
JULIE S.
PENDING

Her pulse stumbled. "He's moving through me again."

Frank caught her shoulders. "Fight it."

"I am."

The room dimmed. Color leeched away until everything settled into sepia tones. The pages of the ledger lifted as though inhaling. Voices poured out, Holmes's smooth cadence layered over Harold's quieter echo.

One records to remember.
One speaks to warn.
Both are the same.

Frank tried to drag her back, but the air pressed against him, thick as water. The pages circled upward, spinning into a column of light. Ink rained from the center, falling in slow, cold drops that burned where they touched skin.

"Dad," Julie gasped. "He's copying me again."

He scanned the desk. A fountain pen lay beside the ledger, twin to the one they'd destroyed. He snatched it and drove it through the page. The ink bled black, then gold, then vanished.

The spiral collapsed. Paper scattered like feathers, whispering as it fell.

For a breath, silence.

Then Harold's voice, clear now, no static. "You can't erase what's set. Only finish it."

Julie turned in a slow circle. "Harold? Where are you?"

"In the margin," he said. "He can't see me here. But he's coming."

The lights flickered. The hum returned, deeper, sharper. Frank felt it in his teeth.

Harold's voice quickened. "You need to leave. The next page is already turning."

They didn't argue. They ran.

Outside, the world had changed again. The air hung heavy with the scent of metal and ozone, the sky boiling but never breaking. Beneath their feet, the street pulsed faintly in time with the radio's forgotten heartbeat. Frank's vision wavered at the edges; the buildings looked ready to collapse inward.

Julie stumbled, catching herself on a lamppost. Her skin burned cold beneath his hand. "He's inside me," she whispered. "He never left."

"Then fight him, Jules."

She looked up, eyes bright with pain. "He says it's easier this way."

Her pupils widened until the gold beneath them flickered like molten script. "You opened the new ledger, Dad. You invited him to continue."

He stepped back, shaking his head. "No. You did that for her. Not for him."

The ground answered before she could speak, a dry tearing sound as the pavement split. Light speared upward, thin as thread.

The light bled upward through the cracks, steady and colorless at first, then brightening until the air itself seemed to hum. Out of it stepped the outline of a man, blurred, unfinished, drawn in motion rather than flesh. Lines of gold ink crawled over the silhouette, sketching features that refused to stay put.

Holmes.

Julie's breath came ragged. "He's not gone," she whispered.

"No," Frank said. "He's rewritten."

The figure smiled without moving its mouth. "Design never dies," it said. "It only changes hands."

Frank grabbed Julie's wrist, but the touch burned. Words beneath her skin flared bright, spilling through his fingers. "He's using me to close it," she gasped.

"Then we end it together," Frank said.

The street vibrated. Windows in the nearest buildings imploded inward, releasing waves of mirrored dust. Harold's voice cut through the chaos, thin but certain. "Frank, listen. There's a way to sever it. Not destruction. Severance. Reflection for reflection, remember?"

Frank looked at Julie. "Change the writer," he murmured.

She nodded once. "Then I become the instrument."

Holmes's form solidified, the ink around him brightening to white. His voice was calm, almost kind. "You can't run from authorship."

Julie took a step forward. "I'm not running."

The ink covering her arms lifted, swirling away in threads of light. Each strand twisted through the air and struck Holmes's chest, burning letters into his shadow. For a heartbeat, their shapes overlapped, his outline wrapped inside hers, both flickering like double exposure.

Harold's voice rose again, faint and breaking. "In the end, every line needs its stop."

Julie's eyes shone silver. "Then this is mine."

She pressed her hand to her heart. Light erupted outward, not blinding but absolute, the kind of brightness that erased sound. For an instant, everything stopped.

Then the world exhaled.

THE DEVIL INSIDE

Silence followed. A soft rain began, though the sky above was still blank white. The city was gone. In its place stretched open fields and the faint shimmer of the lake in the distance. The air smelled of paper after fire.

Frank lay on his side beside the truck, chest heaving. The asphalt beneath him had turned to wet clay, etched with faint spirals like fingerprints. He pushed himself upright. "Jules?"

She sat a few feet away, knees drawn to her chest, breathing hard but alive. The gold script that had covered her arms was gone, replaced by pale scars that looked like the ghosts of words.

He crawled to her. "Are you with me?"

She nodded slowly. "For now."

The wind shifted. Across the empty field, mist gathered above the grass, coiling upward in lazy tendrils. Each wisp shimmered briefly before fading, letters forming, dissolving, never quite making words.

Julie stared. "He's still writing."

Frank followed her gaze. The shapes in the fog pulsed once, twice, then settled into a single faint line:

Observation resumes at dawn.

He reached for her hand. "Then we stay ahead of him."

She squeezed back. "Until the page ends."

They walked toward the truck. Behind them, the mist folded itself flat, leaving the world blank again. Somewhere deep beneath the earth, a single heartbeat echoed, soft, patient, waiting for its next paragraph.

16
THE SOUND AFTER SILENCE

Light collapsed into color, then color into breath.
   Frank didn't remember falling, only the ache afterward. The air tasted scorched, thin, full of static. When he blinked, the world around him trembled, streets half formed, sky pale as worn paper. He sat up slowly, every muscle stiff with something heavier than pain. The last thing he remembered was Julie's voice, sharp and breaking, declaring her final word into creation.

Now there was only silence, and the faint shimmer of golden dust where she'd stood.

"Julie?" His voice cracked, small against the vast stillness. No echo, no wind. Just the world holding its breath.

He stood. The ground beneath him rippled like a reflection on water, each step threatening to collapse into nothing. Buildings leaned in the distance, hollowed by light, their edges rewriting themselves with every blink. It was as if the city hadn't decided what to become yet.

A shape caught his eye, a broken street sign bent backward and flickering between words.

ANNEX
CLOSED UNTIL REVISION.

He swallowed hard. "Harold?"

No answer. Only the soft pulse of the world rebuilding itself one heartbeat at a time.

Julie woke inside the hum.

It wasn't darkness. Darkness implied space. This was absence shaped like a memory. Her breath came slow, each inhale echoing like a line written and erased. When she opened her eyes, she saw herself from a distance, multiple Julies overlapping, each moving a fraction out of sync, all whispering the same unfinished word.

She was inside the ledger. Not the one they'd destroyed, but something born from it.

The pages beneath her skin glowed faintly gold. Words moved there, some hers, some not. Each time she tried to read them, they blurred, reforming into something else. Her father's name appeared once, then vanished, replaced by a phrase she didn't understand:

AUTHORSHIP
TRANSFER IN PROGRESS.

The page beneath her pulsed once, spilling light that shaped itself into lines of handwriting.

She knew that script, the steady, looping letters Harold used in his notes.

Authorship equals observation.
Erase the gaze, erase the god.

The words flickered, then rearranged.

But even erasure leaves residue.

Julie reached toward them, fingertips brushing the glowing ink. It was warm, almost human. She felt the weight of every name that had passed through the ledger, their breaths, their unfinished thoughts, pressing gently against her skin.

"You're still teaching me," she murmured.

For an instant she heard Harold's laugh, soft and weary. Then the script unraveled into dust that drifted upward, and the hum deepened again. Holmes's voice followed, threaded through the fading light.

"You severed the thread, but you didn't close the story."

Julie pressed her hands over her heart. It still beat, faint but real. "Not yet," she whispered. "I'm not done."

The hum deepened, resolving into a voice she recognized too late.

Holmes.

"You severed the thread, but you didn't close the story," he said, his tone patient, indulgent. "You exist between the lines now. That's not living, Julie. It's unfinished."

She turned toward the sound, though there was no direction to face. "You can't control me anymore."

"Can't?" His laugh was soft. "You are the page, my dear. I merely guide the ink."

Her pulse stuttered. But another voice, distant and faint, broke through, her father's, somewhere beyond the emptiness.

"Julie, listen—"

She shut her eyes. "I am."

Frank followed the faint hum threading through the fractured air. The light had dimmed to dusk, though there was no sun. Shadows moved on their own, their sources uncertain. His boots scuffed across broken pavement that flickered between dirt and tile.

He stopped near what had once been a storefront. The glass was gone, replaced by a wall of text, actual sentences etched into light. He leaned closer. They were descriptions of him, written in past tense.

Frank stood before the window, afraid to breathe too loudly.

He wondered if this was Hell, or only its echo.

He stepped back, heart pounding. "Harold," he whispered. "What did we do?"

The reflection in the glass-text shimmered, shifting, not his face now but Harold's, pale and strained.

"You finished the rewrite," the reflection said. "But she's caught in the transition. The ledger's trying to stabilize."

"Then pull her out!"

Harold's image wavered. "I can't. Not from here. But you might."

"How?"

"You were both written into the same sentence."

Frank clenched his fists. "Then I'll change it."

The image smiled faintly, proud and sad. "That's my boy."

Then it vanished.

Julie drifted between paragraphs.

Everywhere she looked, fragments of the world hung suspended, streets half rendered, the lake inverted above her like a ceiling of molten glass. She reached toward it, and her fingers dissolved into light before reforming again. She was thought, half memory, half matter.

Then she heard it, footsteps. Steady. Familiar.

"Dad?"

The hum shivered, twisting around the sound of her voice, carrying it outward. She tried to move toward it, but the air resisted, thick as water. Around her, words began to write themselves in midair, forming columns that swayed like trees in fog.

He's looking for you.

He doesn't remember the ending yet.

Julie's throat tightened. "Then I'll remind him."

She closed her eyes and focused on one thing, his heartbeat. She remembered the way it sounded when he'd held her as a child, when he'd whispered stories to keep the monsters away. She listened now, harder, until the ledger trembled.

The hum faltered.

A crack appeared through the air, thin as a blade of light.

Frank felt it, a pressure shift, the world tilting.

The glow ahead split, releasing a gust of cold air that tasted like ink and rain. Through it, he saw movement, the outline of Julie's hand pressing against nothing.

"Jules!" He ran forward. The air resisted, shattering around him in ripples. He reached the barrier and felt it burn against his palms. The same gold light pulsed beneath his skin, answering hers.

"Dad," her voice echoed, small and distant. "He's rewriting the world. You have to anchor it."

"How?"

Her image flickered, fading in and out like an old film reel. "Find the first line."

"What line?"

"The one he started with," she whispered. "The one he used to call me."

He froze, the answer hitting him like a wound reopening. "Julienne," he said softly. "Before the ledger. Before the name split."

Her expression softened, tears gleaming even through the distortion. "Then say it again."

He did—and the world cracked open.

Light poured through like water breaking a dam. The ledger screamed, pages tearing, rewriting themselves into fragments that rained from the sky. Frank stumbled forward, dragging himself through the collapsing barrier until the air gave way and he fell hard onto solid ground.

Julie lay a few feet away, still glowing faintly. Her eyes fluttered open.

He crawled to her, taking her hand. "Julie," he breathed. "You're here."

She smiled weakly. "Not all of me. But enough."

Around them, the world stabilized. Buildings regained shape. Shadows aligned with light. The road stretched out ahead, ordinary again, except for the faint gold script carved into the asphalt, fading even as they watched.

Frank brushed her hair from her face. "It's over."

She shook her head. "No, Dad. It's written. That's different."

He glanced around. "Where's Holmes?"

Her gaze drifted toward the horizon. "Everywhere there's blank space."

He helped her stand. The ledger's remains lay scattered across the street, each page dissolving into the air like mist. As the last one vanished, the hum finally stopped.

Silence. Real this time.

They walked until the world remembered itself, a roadside, the smell of pine, the whisper of a lake too far to see but close enough to sense. Julie leaned against the truck, her breath shallow but steady. Frank stared at the rising sun, unsure if it was real or just another draft.

"Where do we go now?" she asked quietly.

He looked at her, then at the road ahead. "Anywhere that isn't written."

She smiled. "That sounds impossible."

He managed a small laugh. "So did everything else."

As they climbed into the truck, a breeze moved through the trees, a faint rustle like paper turning. For a moment, Frank thought he heard a voice carried with it, Harold's, maybe, or something older and gentler.

Every story ends where it begins.

He started the engine. "Let's find a new beginning."

The truck rolled forward into the light, and the road behind them folded into silence.

They passed a billboard half hidden by pine needles. The paint peeled in wide curls, exposing bare metal beneath. For a heartbeat it was blank. Then letters bled upward through the rust, slow as dawn:

NEXT EXIT
THE STORY CONTINUES.

Frank blinked. When he looked again, the words were gone. Only streaks of gold remained, running downward like tears.

Julie stared out the passenger window. "The world's resetting itself," she said quietly.

"Or we are," he answered.

Neither of them smiled.

Behind them, the billboard shimmered one last time, faint and deliberate, as if a hand had turned a page.

17
Margins That Still Bleed

The road stretched ahead, too smooth, too new. Asphalt shimmered beneath a colorless sky that refused to choose between dusk and dawn. Frank gripped the steering wheel so tightly his knuckles blanched, afraid that if he loosened his hold even a little, the world might slide back into whatever nightmare they'd just crawled out of.

Beside him, Julie sat silent, eyes half-lidded, her reflection doubled in the window. Every few miles she murmured something under her breath, fragments of sentences that made no sense. "Ink runs forward... he's still writing... turn the page..." Frank wanted to ask what she saw, but every time he opened his mouth, the question died in his throat.

A sign loomed through the haze:

SABLE HOLLOW — 3 MILES.

He'd never heard of it. Yet as the truck crested the hill, a strange déjà vu clawed at the back of his mind. The same trees. The same bend in the road. The same flicker of gold light behind the clouds.

"Almost there," he muttered, though he didn't know why.

Julie's voice was small. "We're not done, are we?"

He glanced at her. Her pupils still carried faint veins of gold, like fine cracks in dark glass. "I don't know, sweetheart. Maybe we just need... rest."

She shook her head slowly. "Holmes doesn't rest. He edits."

The words landed like stones in his stomach.

He turned on the radio to drown the silence, but instead of static, a low hum emerged, heartbeat-steady, familiar, and wrong. Then a whisper cut through the speakers:

The margin isn't closed.

Frank slammed the knob, cutting the power. The hum continued anyway, vibrating through the dashboard, through his bones.

By the time they reached Sable Hollow, dusk had melted into something darker. The town was a skeleton of itself, boarded windows, hollow storefronts, and a fountain in the center of the square that hadn't seen water in decades. Above the cracked stone basin hung a sign in flaking red paint:

WELCOME.

Beneath it, someone had written in black marker:

AGAIN.

Julie stepped out of the truck, hugging her arms against the chill. The air felt wrong, too heavy, like breathing through wet paper. "He's been here," she whispered.

Frank followed her gaze to a storefront with its lights still on. The sign above read:

THE AUTHOR'S BOOKS.

Julie moved before he could stop her. The bell above the door gave a hollow ring that didn't echo. Inside, dust drifted in thick ribbons through the faint amber glow of a single bulb. Books lay open everywhere, on tables, on the floor, some blank, some written in gleaming gold script that seemed to breathe.

Julie crouched, tracing a line across one page. The letters slithered away from her touch, rearranging themselves into new words:

THEY ALWAYS RETURN TO THE QUIET BETWEEN.

"Julie, don't—"

Too late. The bulb overhead flickered violently, then burst.

The air shifted. Reality bent.

The bookstore was gone.

Julie stood in fog so dense it erased everything below her knees. The air smelled of paper rot and rain on old ink. Whispers moved through the mist, faint and familiar, female. The cadence was prayer-like, each voice overlapping another.

She turned slowly, and the fog took shape, an outline forming ahead of her, tall and deliberate. The voice that spoke was soft, courteous.

"Julie."

Holmes.

Her heart pounded. "You're dead."

He stepped closer, half formed, the edges of his body smudged like pencil lines. "No. I'm written. There's a difference."

She backed away. "You can't control me anymore."

A smile cut across his blurred face. "Control? No. I'm simply continuing the narrative you began when you rewrote me."

Something wet hit her cheek. She touched it. Ink. It ran down her face like rain. Beneath it, she heard faint cries, the screams of the women Holmes had killed. They echoed through the fog, merging with the hum that had never stopped.

Holmes lifted his hands, and for the first time she saw what dripped from his fingers: the same black ink, thick and alive, each drop whispering a different name.

Clara.

Margaret.

Annabelle.

The names twisted into the fog, forming ghostly outlines of faces, Holmes's victims, trapped in their own unwritten endings.

Julie's breath hitched. "You murdered them."

His eyes gleamed. "I authored them. There's a difference between killing and composition, my dear."

When he smiled, ink poured from between his teeth.

Frank heard her scream before the world folded.

One second he stood among the books; the next, the same shelves surrounded him again, cleaner, newer, as if untouched by time. He ran outside. The square looked identical. The truck waited. The fountain stood dry.

But the sign overhead read:

WELCOME AGAIN.

The paint was still wet.

He turned in a slow circle. The road stretched into mist, looping back into the square. No matter which direction he faced, the town folded into itself like an unfinished sentence.

"Julie!"

Her voice came from everywhere and nowhere. "He's showing me his victims. He's writing through them."

"Where are you?"

The air shimmered, and she appeared at the end of the street, pale and shaking, her eyes golden, ink bleeding down her cheeks.

"Julie!"

He ran toward her, but halfway there the road rippled and reset. He was back by the truck again. The same shout hung in his throat.

"No," he whispered. "No, no, no."

He drove forward, but every turn brought him back to the square. Each loop left the town darker, smaller, as if reality were erasing itself one rotation at a time.

On the third loop, someone stood in the center of the street.

At first Frank thought it was his reflection, same stance, same posture. Then the man lifted his head, and the smile was wrong. Too precise. Too polite.

Holmes. Wearing his face.

Julie saw them both now, the real Frank, wild-eyed and desperate, and the copy, standing motionless with Holmes's calm precision. The false Frank stepped forward, tilting his head.

"You always trusted your father," he said in Holmes's voice. "Will you trust him now?"

Frank lunged, but the distance between them bent like a reflection in rippling water. He swung at the imposter; his fist passed through air thick with ink. The doppelgänger dissolved and reformed behind him, smile intact.

"You can't kill an author," it whispered. "You only feed the story."

Julie felt something stir beneath her skin, a pulse not her own. The air around her vibrated with the screams of the dead, their voices layering until she could barely stand it.

Then one name rose above the rest.

Margaret.

She recognized the voice. The woman from Holmes's old journals. The one who'd never been found.

"Say it," the echo whispered in her ear. "He can't own what you name."

Julie drew a shaking breath and shouted, "Margaret!"

The world convulsed.

Holmes screamed, not in pain but in fury. The ink that made up his face split into a thousand ribbons, each one carrying a different whisper. The town itself shuddered, its streets unraveling into words that bled gold and black at once.

Frank grabbed Julie, pulling her back toward the truck as the square folded inward. The fountain cracked, spewing ink that caught fire midair. The buildings around them peeled open like paper.

"Run!" he yelled.

They dove into the truck. The engine roared to life on the first try, as if the world wanted them gone. Tires shrieked against melting pavement. Behind them, Holmes's figure towered, half man, half ink, mouth stretched in an endless scream that echoed like turning pages.

The road ahead glowed white.

They drove into it.

When they stopped, night had fallen. The truck idled on a dirt path surrounded by pines. The sign for Sable Hollow was gone. The hum had finally stopped.

Julie leaned her head back against the seat, trembling. "He's not gone."

Frank exhaled, voice low. "No. But he's weaker."

She turned to him. "How do you know?"

He looked down at his hands. They were stained with black ink that didn't come off. "Because he bled this time."

The ink trembled across his skin, alive for one last instant. Tiny letters surfaced, forming shapes he almost recognized, half-words, fragments, the ghosts of sentences. Julie reached out, touching one with her fingertip. The mark pulsed once, rearranging itself into handwriting she knew, Harold's looping script.

Keep going.

It faded into nothing.

Frank stared at the empty space it left behind. "He's still watching," he murmured.

Julie nodded. "Then so is Harold."

Outside, the wind rose, carrying the faint scent of smoke and rain. Somewhere in the distance, thunder murmured again, closer, deliberate, like the turn of a heavy page.

Julie whispered, "Then we'd better keep writing."

Frank nodded, putting the truck in gear. The headlights cut through the mist ahead, illuminating a narrow sign by the roadside. The letters were etched deep into the wood, still wet with ink:

REVISION.

He tightened his grip on the wheel. "Then that's where we're headed."

They drove on. Behind them, the last of Sable Hollow folded into silence.

Far behind them, buried in the dark where the town had been, one word refused to fade—**again**.

18

REVISION

Rain thickened again as the highway unspooled ahead, the engine's hum folding into the rhythm of the storm. Headlights skimmed over a half-buried road sign: MOONLIGHT MOTOR INN – 1 MILE. VACANCY.

Frank drove slower than usual, scanning the darkness ahead. Each mile felt like a heartbeat, steady and nervous. Beside him, Julie sat rigid, staring out at the endless blur of trees. Her skin looked paler under the dashboard light, her reflection ghostlike in the glass.

"You okay?" he asked.

She didn't answer right away. "He's moving again," she said at last. "I can feel it in my chest. He's rewriting space, trying to anchor himself somewhere familiar."

"Holmes?"

She nodded. "He's rebuilding the Castle."

Frank exhaled sharply. "Then we stop him before he finishes it."

The rain intensified as they turned onto a narrow access road. The Moonlight Motor Inn appeared out of the fog like a mirage, its neon sign flickering between red and white, the word VACANCY stuttering into VANISH, just like the motel from before. The parking lot was empty except for one other car, a silver sedan parked crooked near the office.

Frank cut the engine. "We'll rest an hour. Just to—"

Julie's hand clamped around his arm. "He's here."

The air thickened instantly, the temperature dropping ten degrees. Somewhere in the distance, a door creaked open.

The motel lobby smelled of mold and cleaner, bleach layered over something older, dust baked into memory. A man stood behind the counter, reading a ledger by the dim glow of a desk lamp. His suit was outdated, gray, the kind of cut no one had worn since the 1890s.

When he looked up, Frank froze.

It was himself, or rather, the version Holmes had built. Same face, same tired eyes, but the expression was wrong. Collected. Predatory.

"Evening," the fake Frank said, voice smooth and polite. "Need a room?"

Julie's grip tightened on Frank's sleeve. "He's rehearsing."

Frank's throat went dry. "Where is she?"

The imposter's smile widened. "Checking in."

He gestured toward the hallway beyond the office. The wallpaper there was floral and peeling, but beneath the pattern, faint lines of black script pulsed like veins.

Julie took a step forward, gold light flickering faintly in her eyes. "Holmes, stop hiding behind him. You're not rewriting history. You're rotting in it."

The imposter's voice shifted, losing its warmth. "History doesn't rot, my dear. It breathes. It remembers. It repeats."

Then he was gone.

The office light flickered once, and the world blinked.

The motel changed.

Frank stumbled back, shielding his eyes. The floor beneath him wasn't tile anymore. It was wood, polished and blackened by age. Gas lamps lined the corridor, their glass chimneys fogged with soot. The faint hum of electricity was gone, replaced by something else, a steady mechanical rhythm, like gears turning somewhere behind the walls.

Julie whispered, "He's done it. He's rewritten the building."

They walked down the hall, each door numbered in ornate brass. The air was heavy, the smell of iron growing stronger. Faintly, from somewhere above them, came the sound of a woman laughing, bright and nervous, a sound that didn't belong here.

Julie stopped. "That's her. Minnie."

Frank's heart stuttered. "From the ledger?"

"She's alive in the scene. He's remaking the night he killed her."

They found her in Room 207.

The door was open just a crack, and through it candlelight flickered across faded wallpaper. Minnie Williams stood by the mirror, brushing her hair. Her reflection wavered, ghostlike, as though she were made of smoke. She was beautiful, early twenties, soft curls pinned back, her dress a style forty years out of date.

And behind her, fake Frank, Holmes, watched.

He looked perfect. Too perfect. Every line of his face calm, refined, untouched by guilt. He spoke softly, the way a man might speak to a lover he intended to ruin.

"You trust me, don't you, Miss Williams?"

Her reflection smiled faintly. "Of course I do, Henry."

Frank's stomach twisted. He saw the gleam of metal in Holmes's hand, a scalpel glinting like a sliver of moonlight.

Julie whispered, "We can't interrupt the timeline directly. He's writing himself into her death again. If we intervene the wrong way, we become part of it."

"I'm not watching her die."

Frank shoved the door open.

Holmes turned slowly, eyes meeting his. "Ah," he said. "The editor returns."

The air snapped like static. Minnie froze mid-motion, her face blanking into terror.

"Let her go," Frank said.

Holmes tilted his head, examining him. "Do you know what fascinates me, Franklin? You think death ends something. But it doesn't. It simply leaves a blank space."

He moved toward Minnie, the scalpel catching the candlelight. The room stretched, walls lengthening, floorboards bending under impossible gravity. Julie staggered as the script returned to the walls, black ink dripping down like blood.

Frank lunged. Holmes caught his wrist midair, impossibly fast. The scalpel grazed Frank's skin, cold, precise.

Julie shouted something, an incantation or a command, and the gas lamps flared. For a split second, the world flickered between then and now, Victorian elegance shattering into the decayed motel, Minnie's body overlaid with a woman in modern clothes, terrified and alive.

Holmes snarled, voice fractured across time. "She belongs to the page!"

Julie stepped between them, hands trembling but glowing faintly gold. "Then erase me first."

Holmes hesitated.

Frank took the chance and drove the scalpel through the reflection, Holmes's face in the mirror. The glass spiderwebbed with cracks, and the room exploded in light.

When the glow faded, the motel was still again.

Minnie Williams lay on the bed, breathing shallowly, alive. The false Frank was gone, no trace, no blood, nothing but the faint scent of burned ink.

The air shimmered where Minnie's body had been. For a moment, outlines formed in the smoke, other women, pale and flickering. Julie, her hair loose and wet. Clara, holding a single broken key. Pearl, a child of light barely taller than the bedframe. Their mouths did not move, yet the sound that rose was steady and sure, a single word stretched across time.

Remember.

Julie felt the floor pulse beneath her feet. "They're not trapped anymore," she whispered. "They're waking up."

Frank leaned against the wall, gasping. "Then maybe we can glitch him out completely."

Minnie stirred, eyes fluttering open. "Who... who are you?"

Julie smiled softly. "Someone who remembers you."

Tears filled Minnie's eyes. "He promised. He said I'd live forever."

Julie nodded. "You will. But not as his story."

The woman faded, her form dissolving into gold mist that drifted toward the ceiling and vanished.

Frank straightened slowly. "Where'd she go?"

Julie's voice was quiet. "Back to where stories rest when they're finished."

Outside, thunder rolled. The motel shuddered once, then began to crumble, the walls splitting apart to reveal the night sky beyond.

Frank grabbed Julie's hand. "Come on!"

They ran through the collapsing hall. The gas lamps went out one by one. As they burst through the front door, the entire building folded inward, collapsing into a heap of splintered wood and glass.

Behind them, the neon sign of the Moonlight Motor Inn flickered back to life, burning brighter than before.

Only this time, it didn't say VACANCY.

It said:

REVISION COMPLETE.

They stood at the edge of the lot, drenched in rain and silence.

The rain slowed, falling in long silver threads that caught the motel's remaining light. For the first time in hours, nothing moved. No hum. No whisper. Just the thin hiss of water against broken glass.

Frank exhaled, steam rising from his breath. "Maybe it's finally over."

Julie didn't answer. Her gaze stayed fixed on the ruins, where smoke curled upward like breath from a sleeping giant. The smell wasn't fire. It was ink, sharp and metallic, carried by the rain.

Something in that scent turned her stomach. "He's watching," she said softly. "He never leaves the margins empty for long."

Frank followed her eyes. Across the collapsed sign, rain pooled in the grooves of the metal letters, catching reflections of neon still blinking beneath the debris. For a moment, he thought he saw words swimming there, sentences forming and dissolving before he could read them.

The air thickened again. Not with sound, but with presence. A heartbeat so faint it could have been imagined. Then a click, steady and deliberate, the rhythm of an old typewriter somewhere in the distance. Each strike echoed through the wet dark.

Julie flinched. "He's rewriting."

Frank shook his head, forcing calm. "Let him. Every time he rewrites, he bleeds a little more."

Lightning flickered across the clouds, and in that flash she saw Harold's silhouette standing beside the truck, half light, half reflection. He didn't speak. He only lifted a finger to his lips, a gesture of warning or peace. Then he was gone.

The wind shifted. Pages, real pages, yellowed and wet, tumbled from the ruins and skidded across the parking lot. They landed face up near Frank's boots. Each bore a single handwritten line:

THE STORY ENDS WHERE IT BEGAN.

Frank looked at Julie. "That lake again."

She nodded. "He's calling us back."

He wiped rain from his face, feeling cold ink on his palms. "Then we'll finish it where he started it."

They turned toward the truck. The rain eased to a drizzle. When Frank opened the door, he caught his reflection in the rearview mirror. Across the glass, faint letters glimmered, wet and fading:

DRAFT SAVED.

A shiver crawled down his spine. By the time he blinked, the message was gone, washed clean by the rain.

He started the engine. The headlights burned through the mist, painting the road in pale gold. As they drove away, the neon behind them flared one last time, burning brighter than the storm itself.

Julie turned toward the ruins. "He's angry."

Frank nodded. "Good. Let him be."

The hum returned, faint and distant, like a heartbeat buried in the wind.

Julie looked up at him. "You know this isn't over, right?"

He smiled grimly. "It never is."

They climbed back into the truck. The road ahead shimmered faintly in the headlights, twisting through the trees like a sentence yet to be written.

Somewhere behind them, deep in the darkness, Holmes's voice whispered through the rain:

A story only ends when the author stops reading.

Frank turned the ignition. "Then we don't stop."

The truck rolled forward, leaving the ruins of the Castle and the echo of its victims behind.

But in the rearview mirror, the neon sign flickered once more.

REVISION: IN PROGRESS.

19

RESURRECTION DRAFT

The rain eased to a fine mist as new shapes rose out of the fog, structures forming where the motel's ruins had been, boards growing from shadow until a sagging farmhouse stood in their headlights.

"It wasn't here before," Julie said.

They stepped into the cold, mud sucking at their boots. The air carried that same metallic tang of burned paper, the smell the Moonlight Motor Inn had left behind. When they reached the porch, Julie stopped short. Faint gold letters shimmered in the boards beneath their feet:

DRAFT TWO: RESURRECTION.

Frank's stomach sank. "He's been here."

Julie didn't answer. She pushed the door open. It groaned like something waking from a long dream.

Inside, the farmhouse was stripped bare. Wallpaper peeled in long gray ribbons. Furniture lay under a skin of dust. A grandfather clock leaned against the wall, pendulum still, hands stopped at twelve. The air was too cold, an emptiness pretending to be silence.

Frank set his flashlight on the counter, turning a slow circle. "We'll stay until morning."

Julie brushed her fingers across the wall. They came away smudged with ink.

"He's close."

They found the cellar door near the kitchen, a hatch sunk into the floor, its edges ringed with rust. Frank hesitated.

"You think—"

Julie nodded. "It's him."

She pulled the latch before he could stop her. The hinges screamed. A rush of air blew upward, damp and hot, sweet like rotting fruit. The smell was wrong, chemical, artificial, too alive.

They descended.

The beam of the flashlight caught a stainless-steel table, surgical and cold. Around it lay instruments: scalpels, clamps, a saw dulled by rust. Glass jars lined the shelves, each filled with black liquid that gleamed faintly gold at the rim.

Julie whispered, "This isn't the farmhouse."

Frank frowned. "What do you mean?"

She turned the light toward the far wall, brick, Victorian patterning half buried beneath plaster.

"It's his room. He's rebuilding the Castle under the house."

A low hum rose from nowhere, deep enough to shake their ribs.

Frank grabbed her hand. "Julie, we have to go—"

The hum fractured into a whisper.

You brought me home.

The jars trembled. One toppled, shattering. Black fluid spread across the floor, pooling too fast, seeping toward them like a living shadow. The smell of ozone stung their throats.

Frank stumbled back, dragging Julie, but she stopped. Her pupils widened until the gold inside them flickered.

"Do you hear them?" she breathed.

The whisper had become a chorus, Holmes's victims murmuring from inside the walls. Names surfaced between heartbeats. Emeline. Minnie. Clara.

Then another voice layered over them, smooth and precise.

"Franklin. You've done my work for me."

The ink thickened, rising, shaping itself into a man. Lines of smoke became bone, then flesh. A suit formed around him, immaculate. The smile was the same as ever, calm, exact.

Holmes.

"You can't bury a manuscript without readers," he said. "And you two have been devoted."

Julie trembled. "You're not supposed to be alive. You're—"

"A record?" He smiled. "Records are the most persistent form of life."

Frank pulled the scalpel from his coat pocket, the one he'd taken from the motel. "Stay away from her."

Holmes tilted his head, amused. "You misunderstand. I didn't come for her. I came through her."

Heat rippled through the cellar. Julie screamed as gold light burst beneath her skin, pouring through every pore. Holmes's shadow stretched until it touched hers and fused.

Frank lunged. The scalpel struck true, but no blood followed, only ink. Sentences spilled out instead, curling through the air before fading.

Holmes didn't even flinch. "You can't change the hand that holds the pen."

He struck back. Pain exploded across Frank's jaw. The flashlight skittered across the floor, its beam cutting Holmes in half, one side human, the other made of shifting text.

Julie crawled toward Frank, voice shaking. "He's anchoring to the real world. He needs a body."

"Then we don't give him one."

The walls twisted. Pipes burst from brick, coughing steam. Doorways appeared and vanished, each leading into darkness. The air tasted of iron and acid.

Holmes advanced, step by measured step, his voice carrying the weight of every soul he'd claimed. "Every great creation requires a vessel. I built mine once from wood and iron. Now I'll build it from flesh."

Julie snatched the flashlight, throwing its beam into his face. One half looked alive; the other writhed with words. The gold ink pulsed faster, syncing to her heartbeat.

Frank grabbed a jar and hurled it. It shattered, its contents igniting in cold fire, blue edged with gold. Holmes flinched, just enough to prove he could feel.

Julie shouted, "He's tied to his writing. Destroy the sentences."

They ripped at the wallpaper. Underneath, faint lines of text glowed like veins, Holmes's ledger etched into the foundation.

She screamed once.

He admired the precision.

Frank tore the script from the wall. Each rip made Holmes recoil, his body flickering like a broken reel. He lunged, fingers closing around Frank's throat, but Julie smashed another jar across his shoulder. Flames crawled up his arm, devouring the ink. He howled, the sound part human, part wind through steel.

The cellar shuddered. Upstairs, the grandfather clock began to toll.

Holmes staggered, form unraveling. "You think you've won? You think this ends with me?"

Julie stepped closer, eyes shining gold. "No. It ends when you stop writing."

She pressed her glowing hand to his chest.

Light poured outward, searing through him like fire through parchment. Words peeled away, rising into the air and burning out one by one.

Holmes's mouth curved into its final smile. "Then write carefully, my dear. Ink remembers."

He burst apart in white flame.

When the light died, the cellar was still. The table had rusted through. The walls were brick again. Only the clock ticked above them, its pendulum swinging for the first time.

Julie sagged against Frank, shaking. "He's not gone," she whispered.

Frank nodded slowly. Behind the glass face of the clock, faint letters glowed, rearranging themselves like gears:

CHAPTER TWENTY-ONE: PUBLICATION.

He closed his eyes. "Then we finish the book."

Light from the dying fire traced faint scars across the walls, burn marks shaped like sentences. The words pulsed once, then sank back into the brick as though inhaled. The air smelled of ink and rain.

Frank bent to pick up a single page lying at his feet. It was brittle, edges singed, the title scrawled in unfamiliar handwriting:

The Last Experiment.

The rest of the sheet was blank.

Julie watched him fold it carefully and slip it into his coat. "It wants to be written."

He met her eyes. "Then we'll choose the ending this time."

Upstairs, the grandfather clock resumed its slow, patient tick. With every swing the sound changed, metal becoming heartbeat, heartbeat becoming the clack of typewriter keys. Somewhere beyond the walls, the house exhaled, and dust lifted like ash.

They climbed the stairs together. Each step whispered old phrases. Reflection for reflection. Observation resumed.

At the doorway, Frank paused. The farmhouse was rebuilding itself, beams knitting together in reverse, rain flowing upward into the roof. As the door shut behind them, the clock chimed once more. The echo carried through the fog like a printing press coming to life, distant, mechanical, relentless.

For a heartbeat, the air vibrated with static.

Then silence.

20
PUBLICATION

Morning came in fractured color, ashen light leaking through the farmhouse windows, gray and sickly as the smoke that hung over the valley. The rain had stopped, but the air still dripped, dense with fog and the faint hiss of static that never quite faded. Somewhere behind the walls, wires ticked like cooling metal.

Frank sat at the table, staring at the clock. It had stopped ticking at 3:15 a.m. The last chime still seemed to hang in the air, thin as a radio signal just out of range.

Julie leaned against the wall, arms folded tight, her face pale in the half-light. Her skin still glowed faintly where Holmes's shadow had touched her. "It's quieter," she said. "But not gone."

Frank rubbed his temple. "It won't be. Not until we finish him."

"How do you kill something that lives in words?"

He didn't answer. Outside, a car passed on the distant highway, its sound strange, too slow, too deliberate. The world was moving differently now, as if time itself had started reading from a new script.

Julie crossed to the table, turning the small radio she'd found in a cupboard. It sputtered, then caught a signal.

"Police are still investigating the unexplained fire that consumed the Moonlight Motor Inn late last night. No bodies have been recovered. Witnesses describe—"

The reporter's voice stopped abruptly. Another voice took its place.

Smooth. Confident. Smiling even through static.

"I told you the castle was only the beginning."

Julie slammed the radio off. The silence that followed was worse.

"He's in the signal," she whispered. "He's using the airwaves. He doesn't need pages anymore. He has readers."

Frank met her eyes. "Then we cut the feed."

By afternoon they reached town. The fog had followed them, bleaching color from every surface. Billboards shimmered as if they were being freshly printed each second. In a café window, the morning paper glowed behind glass, its headline too bold to belong to this world.

H.H. HOLMES RETURNS.

Frank stopped. "They heard him."

Julie's voice rasped. "He's writing the headlines himself."

As they watched, the ink on the page shifted. The photograph beneath the headline, the familiar grainy portrait of Holmes, blinked. For an instant, his eyes turned toward them.

Julie tore the paper from the display and crumpled it, but faint words bled through her fingers, crawling across the skin of her palm.

Every reader resurrects the author.

Frank grabbed her wrist, wiping at the words. They smeared like wet ink but didn't disappear. "Everyone who reads his name gives him breath."

"Then we stop people from reading it," she said.

"How? We'd have to shut down every screen, every signal—"

The television in the café flickered.

A breaking news segment.

The anchor's smile was too wide.

"He built a house in Chicago," she said, her tone dreamlike. "Rooms within rooms. Corridors that looped back on themselves. Imagine the architecture of fear."

The cadence turned familiar, his words in her mouth. The broadcast cut to static. The café lights dimmed. Every screen on the street went black at once.

Then Holmes's face appeared, no longer historical but alive.

"Thank you for reading," he said softly. "It's good to be remembered."

People screamed.

Back in the truck, the world outside warped into motion blur. Radios in passing cars echoed the same phrase over and over. "It's good to be remembered." Streetlights flickered in sync with his voice. Even the GPS on the dashboard began speaking in Holmes's cadence, recalculating endlessly. "Turn left. The end is closer than you think."

Julie pressed her palms to her ears. "He's printing himself across every signal, turning the world into his page."

Frank gritted his teeth. "Then we go off-grid."

But the compass on the dash spun wildly, pointing nowhere.

They found shelter that night in a roadside church, half collapsed, the roof open to the stars. Candles still stood on the altar, melted nearly to the base. Frank lit one and watched the flame stutter.

Julie wandered down the aisle, fingers brushing across the pews. "I used to think evil needed bodies. Now I think it only needs an audience."

Frank sighed. "Maybe that's all he ever wanted. To be famous forever."

"He's getting it." She turned, her eyes hollow. "You can't erase a story people want to believe."

Before he could reply, the candlelight flickered blue. A sound filled the air, faint at first, then growing louder. Laughter. Polite. Amused. It came from the church speakers, ones that weren't even connected to power.

Then the voice followed.

"Once, they gathered to pray. Now they gather to listen."

The stained-glass windows pulsed with faint light, images shifting, saints replaced by silhouettes in bowler hats, faces blurred.

Julie's breath hitched. "He's here."

Holmes's reflection formed in the altar glass, half man, half distortion. His eyes were steady, his smile charming.

"Franklin," he said. "Julie. You've brought such beautiful attention to my work. Do you know how many people are reading me again? How many voices I speak through?"

The candle flames flared high, stretching into ink-black tongues.

Frank stepped forward. "You think this is life? You're a ghost screaming into static."

Holmes's smile didn't falter. "And yet, you hear me. You believe me. That's all existence requires."

He reached toward the glass. It rippled, thin as water. His hand pressed through. Flesh, not reflection.

Julie screamed. "Frank, he's crossing through!"

Frank hurled the candle, shattering the glass. Shards exploded outward, slicing his arm. The reflection dissolved, but the air where it had been shimmered with heat. The smell of ozone filled the church.

Julie clutched his arm. "He's learning. Every time we stop him, he adapts."

Frank nodded. "Then we stop playing defense."

Billboards displayed no ads now, only text. Sentences, identical and endless, scrolling in gold.

In every city, every lighted window, there's a story waiting to be told.

H.H. Holmes, Author.

Julie counted six before she stopped looking. "He's everywhere."

"Not everywhere," Frank said. "He's got to have a source. A main signal."

She frowned. "You think there's a hub?"

"There has to be. Some transmitter he's anchored to. Maybe—" He stopped.

Ahead, the skyline shimmered, television antennas, radio towers, satellite dishes rising from the hills like iron crosses.

"He's publishing," Julie murmured.

Frank pressed the accelerator. They reached the hill by nightfall. The station's windows glowed faintly, red emergency lights pulsing. The air hummed with power, the kind that made teeth ache.

Inside, monitors lined every wall, each showing a different Holmes, grainy, elegant, smiling straight into the lens.

Some spoke. Others only watched.

Then a low chuckle rolled through the speakers.

"Don't be so dramatic," said a voice behind the light.

Holmes stepped out from between the screens, perfectly real. Frank raised the gun.

"You can't shoot an idea, Franklin," Holmes said pleasantly.

"Watch me."

The shot tore through him, ink and gold spraying the air, then closed, rewritten.

"A clean edit," Holmes mused.

Julie grabbed one of the control panels, ripping cables free. Sparks flew. The lights flickered, but instead of dying, the monitors brightened. Each screen now displayed her face.

Holmes turned toward her. "Ah. My finest collaborator."

"Not anymore," she hissed.

Julie seized the microphone linked to the transmitters.

"If you can hear my voice," she shouted, "turn it off. Every screen, every signal. He lives through attention."

Holmes laughed. "Fear counts as attention, my dear. You've just gone viral."

Frank smashed the control board. Sparks erupted, flooding the room with white. Julie gripped the mic, her voice breaking through the feedback. "Then listen to this—"

She threw the master switch.

Silence.

For a moment there was nothing. No hum. No voice. No ink.

Frank lowered the gun. "Did it work?"

Julie stared at the blank monitors. "I don't know."

Then the nearest screen flickered. Just once.

Holmes's face appeared for half a heartbeat, burned and smiling.

"Every ending's just a deadline," he whispered.

The screen shattered.

Outside, dawn rose red. The city below shimmered faintly, as if the skyline were still remembering itself.

Julie stood at the railing, staring into the haze. "He's not gone."

Frank joined her. "Then we keep writing."

She nodded slowly. "We make our own ending."

The wind picked up, carrying scraps of burnt paper from the hilltop, each piece etched with fading gold script:

THE DEVIL INSIDE.
SECOND EDITION.

21

SYNDICATION

The world didn't end when the screens went dark.

It just learned how to keep watching in the dark.

The first morning after the Broadcast, news anchors spoke in careful tones, their eyes glassy and distant. Networks across the country aired the same opening line, word for word:

"We interrupt our regular programming to revisit the events of last night."

Clips replayed of the flickering image, the voice that shouldn't have existed, the face reconstructed from history. Holmes smiled from every channel, every feed, every social post that hadn't yet been deleted. In one loop, his lips moved out of sync with the words, as though the broadcast had been spliced together from a hundred separate realities.

Twitter trended #TheHolmesBroadcast within hours. Some viewers called it a deepfake. Others called it a haunting. But most, far too many, called it performance art.

By midday, talk show hosts were quoting him.

"He built a house of fear," one said. "Isn't that what all great writers do?"

Another laughed, nervously. "If you think about it, he predicted our obsession with true crime before it existed."

The laughter never quite reached their eyes.

A day later, streaming services began receiving anonymous uploads, grainy footage of an old man in a bowler hat walking through crowds, always a few seconds behind the camera operator. Police couldn't trace the source.

And every night, around 3:15 a.m., when the original broadcast had ended, the signal returned briefly. One frame of static. Then a whisper.

"Thank you for tuning in."

By the end of the week, the phrase appeared on billboards, subway ads, even printed receipts. Not all of them were digital. Some were handwritten in the same elegant, slanted cursive that had haunted the margins of Holmes's ledgers.

Society called it The Holmes Effect. Psychologists called it mass hysteria.

Julie called it something else.

"Publication," she said.

They had moved again, farther into the hills. The farmhouse had collapsed into itself overnight, the air still smelling of ash and ink. Now they stayed in a hunter's cabin, barely a structure at all, a shell of cedar leaning against the wind.

Frank sat by the small fireplace, tuning a battery-powered radio with shaking fingers. Each channel he landed on eventually echoed the same faint hum beneath the static, as though the entire world now shared one heartbeat.

Julie watched him from the doorway. Her hair hung loose, damp from rain. She looked like she hadn't slept in days.

"He's everywhere," she said softly. "You can't tune him out anymore. He's in the words themselves."

Frank turned the dial sharply. "No. He's a parasite. He needs attention to live. That means he can die."

Julie shook her head. "You can't kill an idea."

"Then we find where it's writing from and burn it out."

He gestured toward the small television they'd salvaged from an old convenience store. The screen flickered, faint and gray, then stabilized on a newsfeed. The anchor's voice was calm, too calm.

"Authorities confirm the discovery of an unidentified body outside the ruins of the Moonlight Motor Inn. No identification has been made, but sources report the initials 'H.H.' carved into the surrounding wood."

Julie's breath caught. "He's marking the world again."

Frank muted the sound. "Then he's trying to rebuild his story. Physically this time."

She sank into the chair beside him. "He's writing sequels."

He laughed bitterly. "He never knew when to stop."

She looked at him, serious. "Neither do we."

Night fell heavy. Wind clawed at the walls, carrying the sound of something distant, voices maybe, echoing off the ridgeline.

Julie lay awake on the cot, staring at the ceiling. In her mind, the broadcast replayed again and again. Holmes's smile. His words. The feeling of being watched even after the screens went black. She could still hear him when she closed her eyes.

Julie, you gave me language. I gave you immortality.

She sat up, heart pounding. "Frank?"

He stirred beside the dying fire. "Yeah?"

"Do you hear him?"

He hesitated. "Sometimes."

"He's looking for me."

Frank rose slowly. "He can't reach you without a medium."

"The world is the medium now."

The window rattled. Both of them turned. A figure stood outside in the fog, just beyond the glass, tall and motionless. Its outline was blurred by mist, but the hat was unmistakable.

Frank grabbed the flashlight and lunged toward the door, flinging it open. The night was empty. Only the smell of ozone remained.

Julie's voice trembled. "He's testing the distance."

The next morning brought new horror.

Radio hosts were reading entire paragraphs from Holmes's supposed journals. "Anonymous sources," they called them. Listeners sent recordings of whispers bleeding into their phone lines, Holmes's voice repeating fragments from his past interviews, now adapted into perfect, modern phrasing.

"Murder, dear listeners, is only a form of punctuation."

Some stations tried to censor the phrase. Others used it as a tagline.

Julie and Frank drove into town at dusk, their gas running low. The streets were too quiet. Storefronts stood open but abandoned. In a café window, a television played without sound. Inside, three people sat frozen, eyes wide, faces turned toward the screen.

Frank stepped closer.

The anchor was smiling again. "Tonight, we explore how the line between killer and creator continues to blur. Who writes the ending of a life?"

Julie touched the glass. The reflection didn't match her. Her mirrored self smiled faintly and whispered, "You already know."

THE DEVIL INSIDE

She jerked her hand back. "He's writing through reflections."

Frank nodded grimly. "And the audience keeps giving him ink."

They turned to leave and froze.

Across the street, an entire billboard was changing, letters crawling over its surface like living worms. The message formed slowly, deliberately:

TO BE CONTINUED.

Frank's heart hammered. "He's serializing himself."

Julie whispered, "Then we end the series."

They returned to the cabin before dark. Julie began collecting their notes, the journal entries, and every scrap of ledger pages they'd salvaged from the motel.

Frank poured gasoline over the pile. "If attention is life, then ignorance is death."

Julie hesitated. "He'll fight it."

"Let him."

He struck the match.

The fire roared to life, bright gold, the pages curling instantly into ash. The smoke rose thick, swirling into symbols, Holmes's handwriting, his words trying to reassemble themselves midair.

A true author never dies between editions.

Frank threw the rest of the gas onto the flames. The words twisted, screamed, then vanished.

Julie covered her face, coughing. "Do you think it's enough?"

Frank looked toward the horizon, where the fog seemed to pulse faintly in time with the wind. "We'll find out tomorrow."

By midnight, the fire was gone. The radio had gone silent for the first time in days. Julie drifted into uneasy sleep.

Frank sat alone by the ashes, staring at the empty air.

The quiet felt unnatural, like holding his breath inside someone else's dream.

Then he heard it, faint, from outside. The sound of shuffling feet.

He stood, weapon ready, and stepped to the door.

The forest beyond the porch was motionless.

Until something stepped out of the trees.

A man. Ordinary clothes. But his eyes were gray and familiar.

Frank froze. "Sir, you lost?"

The man smiled slowly. "No." His voice was smooth, confident. "Just following a story."

He lifted his hand. In his palm, etched like a scar, were the initials H.H.

Frank stumbled back. "Jesus Christ."

The man's smile widened. "Close enough."

Behind him, others appeared, shapes moving in the mist, faces half recognizable, all speaking in the same even tone.

"Good evening, Franklin."

"We've read your work."

"We'd love to see how it ends."

Julie woke to the sound of voices. She bolted upright, eyes wide. "Frank?"

He turned toward her, voice shaking. "He's not in the air anymore."

The crowd advanced, hundreds of silhouettes forming from fog and rain, each whispering the same word in perfect unison.

"Read."

Julie grabbed his arm. "He's turned them into pages."

THE DEVIL INSIDE

Frank stared at the endless gray horizon. The entire valley shimmered faintly with golden text, lines crawling across the mist itself.

"Then we burn the book," he said.

Julie looked at him, understanding. "Everything?"

"Everything."

He lit the last match and dropped it on the floor.

The flames caught fast. The cabin ignited around them, smoke curling into words that dissolved as soon as they formed. Outside, the fog hissed, recoiling like a wounded animal.

Holmes's voice rose one last time, scattered, desperate.

"You can't erase the reader!"

Julie whispered, "We're not. We're rewriting them."

She pressed her palm to Frank's, gold light flaring between them. The fire turned white.

And then silence.

Morning came.

The hill was nothing but ash and soil. No cabin. No pages. No sound except the wind.

At the edge of the field, a single object remained half buried, a cracked mirror, its surface faintly glowing.

For a heartbeat, a reflection moved inside it. A man's smile, elegant and patient.

Then the glass shattered.

22

THE RESIDUALS

The fire burned itself out by dawn.

Smoke curled through the trees, heavy and gray, turning the hills into silhouettes. Where the cabin had stood was now nothing but ash, warped metal, and the faint outline of a door burned into the soil.

Frank stood barefoot in the wet grass, his clothes scorched, his skin raw. Every breath tasted like cinders. Behind him, Julie crouched near the ruins, sifting through the blackened earth with trembling hands. She was alive, barely. The light that had saved them both was fading from her skin, replaced by bruises and soot.

He said her name once, softly.

She didn't look up. "He's not gone."

Frank wiped blood from his lip. "I know."

She held up a fragment of something that hadn't burned. A strip of paper, edges singed but intact. Letters gleamed faintly across it, Holmes's handwriting unmistakable.

Post Office Annex, Chicago.

Her eyes met his. "He's calling us home."

They walked for hours down the mountain road, the world still thick with fog. No cars passed. No birds sang. It was as if nature itself was holding its breath.

When they reached a gas station, the television behind the counter glowed with static. The attendant didn't move when they entered. His eyes were open, his mouth slack, as though frozen mid-conversation.

Julie waved a hand in front of his face. Nothing.

Frank turned toward the TV. The static shifted. For an instant, an image flickered through, the shape of a man in a bowler hat, smiling faintly. Then gone.

"Residual," Julie whispered. "Like an echo of him."

Frank grabbed two bottles of water and a road map from the counter. He left cash on the table, though no one asked for it. "We head east. Chicago's the root."

Julie nodded. "If we destroy where he began, we end the cycle."

They stepped outside. The attendant blinked once and looked around as if waking from a dream. "Y'all heading somewhere?" he called after them.

Frank didn't answer.

They drove for two days, sleeping in the truck when they couldn't keep their eyes open. Every town they passed looked wrong, signs repeating themselves, streetlights blinking in unnatural rhythm.

Somewhere in Iowa, the radio caught a faint signal. Julie turned the dial carefully, and a man's voice slipped through the static.

"Welcome back to our continuing series on H. H. Holmes, America's first storyteller of death."

She switched it off immediately. "He's rewriting the airwaves again."

Frank stared at the road ahead. "He's not writing anymore. The world is writing for him."

She leaned against the window, eyes half-closed. "Then we take the pen away."

Chicago appeared through a haze of rain and distant thunder. The skyline was a smudge of steel and shadow, windows flickering with ghostlight. They crossed into Englewood by evening, the streets quiet and damp, the city holding the weight of its own forgotten history.

Frank parked near 63rd and Wallace. The Post Office loomed across the street, a hulking red-brick building from the 1930s, its windows dark, its doors chained shut.

Julie stared at it, breath shallow. "This is it."

Frank's gaze followed hers. "Where the Castle stood."

The last of the daylight faded. The building seemed to breathe, the bricks shifting under the glow of the streetlamps. Faint words began to appear on the facade, written in water and shadow.

Property of the Author.

Julie's hand trembled as she reached for the door. "He's still buried here."

Frank stopped her. "Not buried. Bound."

They slipped through a broken side window into a corridor lined with filing cabinets and dust. The air was stale and cold. Somewhere deep in the building, a steady dripping echoed like a metronome.

Julie whispered, "He used the basement for his furnaces."

Frank nodded. "And now it's his tomb."

They found the stairs behind a steel maintenance door. The padlock had already been cut, rusted metal curling like paper.

Each step downward felt heavier, the temperature dropping with every foot.

The basement stretched wider than it should have, hallways branching off in directions that didn't fit the blueprints Frank had studied years ago.

A low hum vibrated through the floor.

Julie lifted her flashlight. "Do you hear that?"

Frank frowned. "It's not electricity."

They followed the sound into a vast, circular chamber. The walls were brick, old and slick with condensation. In the center stood a steel table, rusted but intact.

The same table from the farmhouse cellar.

Julie's breath hitched. "He's rebuilding the Castle in layers, everywhere he's existed."

Frank approached the table. Something lay on it, a bound book, its cover blackened with soot. The ledger.

He reached for it. Julie grabbed his wrist. "Don't."

"He left it for us."

"Or for himself."

He hesitated, then flipped it open.

The pages were blank except for one line written in gold ink across the center:

The story ends where the first body fell.

Frank looked up sharply. "That's not here."

Julie shook her head slowly. "No. It's deeper."

She turned toward the far wall. Beneath the grime, a door outline shimmered faintly, etched in gold. She pressed her palm against it. The metal shuddered.

The hum rose.

A whisper seeped through the cracks.

"Welcome home."

The door swung open.

The room beyond was impossibly clean. Tile floor. White walls. Fluorescent lights that shouldn't have worked. The air was warm, clinical. In the center stood a glass case containing a single object, a scalpel, preserved and gleaming.

Julie stepped closer. "That's his."

Frank felt a chill crawl up his spine. "It's more than that."

He looked at the floor. Names were etched into the tiles, Holmes's victims. Some real. Some new. At the end of the list:

Julie S.

Pending.

She went still. "The tiles are changing under my feet again."

The lights flickered.

A voice filled the room, not loud, but everywhere.

"You can't erase what the world has accepted."

Holmes's reflection appeared on the glass of the case, smiling.

Julie's voice trembled. "Then we make the world forget."

The reflection blinked. "Impossible."

Frank met his gaze. "We'll rewrite the writer."

Holmes's smile faltered. For the first time, doubt crossed his perfect face.

The lights shattered.

They ran as the floor cracked open, the tiles splitting into rivers of molten gold. The entire basement shook. Somewhere above them, alarms began to wail, but the sound warped, each siren note stretching into distorted laughter.

Frank grabbed Julie's hand, dragging her toward the stairs. The air pulsed like a living thing, words crawling along the walls in burning ink.

AUTHORS NEVER DIE.
READERS MAKE THEM IMMORTAL.

They reached the corridor, but the exit had sealed itself in shadow. Behind them, the ledger lay open on the floor, its pages flipping wildly.

Julie turned, eyes blazing. "We can still close it."

Frank looked at her. "How?"

"We rewrite his first moment. Where it started."

He stared, realization dawning. "The basement isn't the beginning."

She nodded. "The furnace is."

They ran deeper into the darkness, following the heat. The hum turned into a roar.

At the far end of the hall, they found it, a massive incinerator, its mouth wide open, glowing faintly gold. Flames licked the edges of reality itself.

Julie raised her hands, gold light surging from her skin once more. "Every page burns."

Frank threw the ledger into the furnace. The moment it touched the fire, the entire room erupted in light.

Holmes's voice screamed through the heat, shattering into fragments.

"You can't unwrite me!"

Julie stepped closer, shouting over the roar. "Then we'll make you forgotten!"

The flames consumed everything, the words, the walls, the sound.

Frank reached for her hand one last time as the fire swallowed them both.

When the light faded, the basement was silent.

The incinerator stood cold and empty. The ledger was gone. The gold writing on the walls had vanished.

Outside, morning broke over Chicago. The Post Office was just a building again, quiet, ordinary, and forgettable.

But under its foundation, in the ash of the furnace, something stirred once before falling still.

A single word remained carved into the brick:

Erase.

23

The Revision Ritual

The air still shimmered with heat. The incinerator's mouth was black now, its glow long faded, but the smell of burnt metal and ink lingered in every breath. Frank stood before it, one hand braced on the wall to steady himself. His skin was streaked with ash, his eyes hollowed by exhaustion and smoke.

Julie crouched beside the furnace, tracing the last word left in the soot.

Erase.

She whispered it aloud, and the sound wavered like a candle flame. "It isn't over. He's still here, just beneath the page."

Frank stared into the dark mouth of the incinerator. The gold veins once threaded through the brick now pulsed faintly, like blood under cooling skin. "He's feeding on what's left of him," he said. "Memory."

Julie rose slowly, the light within her flickering weakly. "Then we stop remembering."

Frank turned to her. "That's not possible."

"It has to be," she said. "He doesn't exist without witness. We're the last ones who know how this began. If we end that knowledge, we end him."

He frowned. "You're talking about erasing ourselves."

Julie met his gaze. "I'm talking about rewriting him out of us."

The sub-basement stretched farther than it should have. The corridors no longer obeyed the laws of the building above. They bent inward, folding like paper. At the far end, where light refused to hold, a faint gold circle glowed on the floor. Symbols crawled across it like ink spreading through parchment.

"The ledger's roots," Julie murmured. "It's still alive down here."

Frank stepped closer, studying the pattern. Each line curved into a word, and each word formed a name, Holmes's victims etched in a loop that never ended. In the center was his own.

Franklin.

The voice came from everywhere at once, low and even, as if it were spoken from inside their heads.

Holmes's reflection appeared in the air. No body now, only the outline of one, drawn in light and smoke. His bowler hat was gone. His eyes burned molten gold.

"You've come so far to meet me again," he said softly. "Do you understand what I am yet?"

Julie clenched her fists. "A story."

Holmes smiled. "A truth. Every story that's told enough becomes one."

Frank stepped into the circle. "You're a ghost of your own myth. And like every myth, you end when no one believes."

Holmes tilted his head. "Belief is the easiest thing to rewrite."

The symbols around the circle began to twist, letters reversing themselves, forming new words in a language neither of them recognized. The air grew heavier.

Julie took a step forward, her hands trembling with gold light. "Then we write it better."

The floor cracked beneath them. The circle collapsed inward, pulling them into darkness.

Frank landed hard on stone. No longer the basement floor, but a corridor lined with gas lamps. The Murder Castle reborn, flawless and cruel. The walls pulsed with veins of gold script, each word alive.

Julie stood beside him, her breath catching. "He's rebuilt it from our memories."

Holmes's voice echoed down the hall.

"Every revision requires a setting. Every death deserves a stage."

He appeared ahead of them, fully formed now, flesh and suit immaculate. He looked alive.

Julie felt her heart race. "You can't be here."

He smiled. "You brought me back. Every retelling, every desperate attempt to destroy me, kept me inked."

Frank lifted the scalpel he'd carried since the motel. "Then this is the last telling."

Holmes spread his arms, gracious. "Then write your ending."

They charged.

Holmes caught Frank by the throat mid-swing, slamming him against the wall. The brick turned soft, absorbing him like clay. Julie screamed and thrust her hand forward, a surge of golden light bursting from her palm. Holmes staggered, his outline flickering, but he didn't fall.

"You still use my ink," he hissed. "You can't kill me with my own creation."

Julie gritted her teeth. "Then I'll unmake it."

She reached into the air and tore a word from the wall, an actual word, luminous and writhing. It screamed as she crushed it between her hands. The corridor convulsed. Lamps shattered. The castle's architecture rippled like a disturbed reflection.

Frank broke free, gasping, his skin marked by words that faded as quickly as they appeared. "Keep going!"

Julie grabbed another string of letters and ripped them apart. Each one dissolved into dust.

Holmes screamed, his voice multiplied a hundredfold. "You're erasing meaning! You'll destroy everything!"

"That's the point!" she shouted.

Light burst through the cracks in the walls, faces surfacing in the fire, the women he'd claimed. Julie's eyes opened first, then Minnie's, then a chorus of others, their features stitched from flame and ink. They were not ghosts now but memories made sovereign, each holding a fragment of the words Julie had written.

"He used us to build his story," Julie said, her voice layered with all the others. "Now we'll write him out."

The fire surged toward Holmes, gold turning white. He stumbled as the voices rose, a harmony of defiance, every syllable tearing a piece of him apart.

The corridor collapsed around them. They fell again, landing in what looked like a library, floor-to-ceiling shelves filled with identical books. Every spine read the same title.

The Devil Inside.

Julie spun, horrified. "He's rewritten the story into infinity."

Holmes's laughter filled the air, gentle, elegant.

"A proper author never stops creating."

Frank grabbed one of the books and tore it open. The pages were blank.

Julie frowned. "Why are they empty?"

Holmes appeared beside her, whispering near her ear. "Because they're waiting for your ending."

She turned and drove her fist through his chest. Her hand met smoke. He vanished.

Frank's voice came from behind her. "Julie. The books, look."

The shelves were disintegrating. Each blank page burned from the inside out, gold light bleeding through the paper like fire behind frost.

Julie realized what it meant. "He's losing control."

Frank nodded. "Finish it."

At the center of the library stood a single desk, the one Holmes had used in his Chicago office, recreated perfectly. On it sat a single blank ledger and a pen of solid gold.

Julie approached it slowly. "This is where he began."

Holmes appeared across from her, half his face burned away. "You think you can rewrite me?"

She met his gaze. "No. I'm writing without you."

Frank stepped behind her, resting a hand on her shoulder. "Do it."

She dipped the pen into the air, drawing light instead of ink, and began to write on the page. The words burned as she formed them.

This is not his story.
This is the absence of him.

Holmes roared, lunging forward, but Frank caught him, wrestling him back as the words multiplied across the page. Each sentence dissolved a piece of him. His voice fractured, falling apart mid-syllable.

"You can't delete me—"

Julie wrote faster, tears streaking her face.

He was never written.
He never existed.
The author has no name.

The pen blazed white-hot, melting in her fingers. The pages burst into flame. Holmes screamed one last time, a sound of pure static, and vanished, ink, smoke, and memory collapsing inward until nothing remained but silence.

The castle disintegrated around them, walls folding into paper, paper dissolving into dust.

When the light dimmed, Frank and Julie stood once again in the basement beneath the Post Office. The incinerator was gone. The air was clean, still, and empty.

Somewhere in that silence, a child's voice hummed, a faint, tuneless melody carried on the settling dust.

Julie froze. "Did you hear that?"

Frank listened. Only air moved.

But she knew the sound. She'd heard it once in a dream, before all of this began.

Pearl's lullaby.

The sound lingered a heartbeat longer, then unraveled into nothing, leaving only stillness.

Julie smiled faintly. "She's free too."

She dropped the ruined pen. "Is it over?"

Frank looked at the wall. No writing. No hum. No residue. "I think it is."

They turned toward the stairs. As they climbed, sunlight filtered down through cracks in the ceiling.

By the time they reached the surface, the city was alive again. Normal. Buses, traffic, laughter. The world had moved on.

Julie looked up at the sky. "Do you feel it?"

Frank smiled faintly. "Peace?"

She shook her head. "Forgetting."

They walked together into the morning.

Inside the sub-basement, one fragment of the burnt ledger drifted through the air before settling on the cold floor. The faintest trace of handwriting shimmered, then vanished.

Then silence.

True and final.

24

THE FINAL DRAFT

Morning unfurled over the city like a page turned too softly to hear. The light was clean for the first time in years, no hum in the air, no shimmer of gold ink crawling across the skyline. Chicago breathed again. Cars moved. People laughed. The world, unaware of what it had lost, moved forward.

Frank stood on the steps of the Post Office, watching the steady rhythm of life return. Delivery trucks idled. Pigeons gathered near the loading dock, pecking at crumbs. He could smell coffee from a cart down the street. For the first time since the lake, nothing smelled like ink or ash.

Julie joined him, wrapping her arms around herself against the chill. The wind tugged at her hair. She looked tired but calm, the faint glow in her skin finally gone.

"No one remembers him," she said quietly.

Frank nodded. "That's the point."

"It feels wrong."

He turned to her. "You'd rather they lived with him haunting their heads?"

Her mouth twisted in a small, weary smile. "Maybe I just don't like being the only one who knows."

Frank looked at the crowd across the street, faces bright and unshadowed. "They're free. That's enough."

They started walking. The city sounded different now, lighter, almost fragile. Billboards were blank, their white surfaces waiting for new stories. Street signs flickered once, resetting names. The whole world seemed to have exhaled.

Julie stopped at a newsstand. The headlines were mundane, elections, markets, weather, but one front page caught her eye: *Historic Post Office Fire: Officials Cite Faulty Wiring.*

No mention of Holmes. No history, no legacy, not even myth.

She traced the edge of the paper. "He's really gone."

Frank took her hand. "So are the others. The ones he wrote into pain."

Julie glanced up. "And us?"

He didn't answer. Not yet.

They rented a car and drove north. The radio played nothing but static, but it was clean, empty static, not haunted hum. Outside the city, the sky opened wide, blue and heavy with late-afternoon light.

Julie watched the horizon. "It's strange," she said. "To win by disappearing."

"You haven't disappeared."

"Haven't I?" She smiled faintly. "We burned everything we were. Our names are probably gone too."

Frank tightened his grip on the steering wheel. "If the world forgot us to forget him, that's a fair trade."

They passed through towns that looked untouched, new in subtle ways, like someone had rewritten their history just slightly kinder. The gas station attendant in Iowa didn't recognize them. No one did. Even the motel clerk who handed them a room key seemed distant, mechanical, as if their presence didn't fully register.

They were ghosts in a world reborn.

That night, Julie sat by the window, the motel's neon glow painting her face pink and blue. Frank watched her reflection in the glass, the way her eyes caught the light.

"What are you thinking?" he asked.

She hesitated. "If a story ends and no one remembers it, does it really end?"

"Yes," he said. "Because we were there to make sure it did."

Julie's gaze drifted to the reflection again. "I keep waiting for the hum."

"It's gone."

"You sure?"

He nodded, but his hand found hers anyway. "Even if it isn't, it can't write without us."

They sat in silence until dawn. The neon sign outside flickered once, then steadied.

Weeks passed. They traveled without purpose, crossing state lines like ghosts in borrowed bodies. They stopped in diners, on backroads, at lakesides. Each place felt too ordinary, too unburdened. The horror had left the world clean and fragile.

One evening, they found themselves outside a small library in Michigan. Julie paused at the entrance, staring at the marble plaque by the door:

Dedicated to the Memory of Those Whose Stories Remain Untold.

Something in the words pulled at her.

THE DEVIL INSIDE

Inside, the shelves were quiet. She wandered until she reached the history section. Her hand skimmed across titles, serial killers, true crime, American folklore. Holmes's name was nowhere. Not in the indexes. Not even as a footnote.

She turned to Frank. "He's really been erased. Like he never existed."

Frank smiled softly. "That's what we wanted."

She hesitated. "But what happens to a story when it's gone? Does the void stay empty?"

He thought for a moment, then said, "Maybe it fills with something better."

Julie nodded, but her eyes lingered on the empty space between the books, the gap where history used to be.

They settled for a time near Lake Superior, in a cabin Frank rented under a false name he barely remembered choosing. The air was cold and clean. The water stretched forever, gray and beautiful, the horizon fading into sky.

Julie spent her days walking the shoreline, collecting smooth stones. Frank wrote, not stories, just notes. Lists. Thoughts. Words to keep his hands moving. He didn't know if the world would let ink remember him.

One evening, she found him at the table, staring at a blank page.

"What are you writing?"

He looked up. "Nothing. Maybe everything."

She smiled. "That's how it starts."

Frank set the pen down. "I'm tired of stories."

"Then don't tell one," she said. "Just live one."

They stepped outside together. The sky glowed orange, the lake catching every hue like polished metal. Julie leaned against him. For a moment, the silence was perfect.

Then the wind shifted. A whisper moved across the water, soft, almost inaudible.

Julie's pulse quickened. "Did you—"

Frank held up a hand. "Wait."

The whisper faded, replaced by the natural sound of waves. Just water. Just wind.

He smiled. "Not everything is a ghost."

Julie let out a shaky laugh. "You sure?"

"Yeah." He slipped an arm around her. "For once."

Winter came early that year. The lake froze by mid-November, the horizon a sheet of silver. Julie stood outside one morning, breath fogging the air. She drew a single word in the frost on the window:

End.

Frank joined her, reading it quietly. "It's fitting."

She nodded. "Every story needs a period."

He took her hand and pressed it gently against the glass. The word melted under their touch, disappearing back into water.

They stood in silence for a long time, the cold biting at their skin but not their peace.

Months later, when the snow began to thaw, Frank woke to an odd stillness. The house was too quiet. He found Julie outside, sitting on the porch steps, watching the sunrise. Her expression was peaceful, distant but calm.

She turned as he joined her. "It's fading," she said.

"What is?"

"The memory." She smiled faintly. "Of him. Of everything. Even us."

Frank sat beside her, heart heavy. "That's the cost."

"I know." She leaned her head on his shoulder. "It's a good cost."

The sun climbed higher, painting the frozen lake in gold. He closed his eyes. For the first time, he couldn't recall the sound of Holmes's voice.

He whispered, "We did it."

Julie nodded. "We took his name out of everything."

By summer, the cabin stood empty. Locals said it had been abandoned for years. No one remembered who built it or who stayed there.

But sometimes, on clear evenings, hikers along the shore would swear they saw two figures standing by the water, a man and a woman side by side, watching the horizon.

No one ever saw their faces.

Back in Chicago, the basement beneath the Post Office remained sealed. The workers spoke of strange echoes and whispers when the wind came from the lake, but no one investigated.

In the corner of the foundation, a single brick glowed faintly gold when the light hit it just right. Beneath the surface, one last word remained carved, almost too faint to read:

Peace.

Not forgotten.

Not rewritten.

Simply left unwritten, where even monsters can't return.

And above it, silence.

Real, human silence.

The kind that doesn't hum.

The kind that means it's over.

Epilogue

After the Silence

Years later, the lake looked the same.

Water met sky in a soft gray seam, and the world breathed without remembering why. The shore was quiet except for the steady sigh of waves and the wind threading through the reeds.

A boy wandered there one morning, shoes damp with dew. His family was camping farther inland, and he'd woken before the others, drawn by the whisper of the water. He was maybe ten, the age when curiosity still outweighed fear. Near a line of driftwood, something half buried caught his eye, a scrap of paper, weathered and soft, its edges frayed by time. He pulled it free carefully.

It wasn't blank.

A few faint words glimmered across it, written in gold so pale it could have been sunlight.

The world remembers the quiet that came after.

He turned it over. Nothing else. No title. No creator.

The boy smiled, not sure why. He tucked the page into his pocket and walked back toward camp, whistling a tune he couldn't name and wouldn't remember.

THE DEVIL INSIDE

Behind him, the wind rose, lifting small waves onto the shore. For an instant, the foam traced patterns that almost looked like handwriting before dissolving back into water.

In the city, the old Post Office still stood. Most people passed it without a glance, its walls faded and ordinary. The building had no plaques, no legends, no stories attached.

But every spring, when the light hit just right, a faint warmth stirred deep beneath the floor, nothing unnatural, only the ordinary heartbeat of a world allowed to remember kindness instead.

Workers swore that on quiet mornings, the hum of machinery sounded almost like breathing, peaceful, steady, human.

Far from there, an old notebook sat on a shelf in a forgotten library. Its cover was plain, unmarked. No one knew who had written it, or when, or why the pages inside were blank.

Except for one.

Near the center, in fine handwriting, a single line curved across the page:

Every story ends when it's finally heard.

No one borrowed the book.
No one remembered placing it there.

But sometimes, in the half light before closing, the librarian swore she could feel a draft move across the room, warm, faintly perfumed with rain and smoke, and two shadows standing near the window, watching the world they'd rewritten.

On clear nights, the wind across the lake sometimes carried faint laughter, not fearful, but free.

One tall.
One small.
Both still.

BARB JONES

At peace.

About The Author

Barb Jones is a literary force to be reckoned with, captivating readers worldwide with her best-selling and award-winning Blood Prophecy and Heaven and Hell series. An acclaimed author in the realms of supernatural thrillers and horror, she crafts gripping narratives that linger long after the last page is turned. Holding advanced degrees in Accounting, Finance, and Information Technology, Barb seamlessly blends her analytical prowess with her creative genius, resulting in stories that are both intellectually stimulating and thrillingly entertaining. With multiple accolades to her name, she writes not just for herself, but for her dedicated readers, delivering spellbinding tales that keep them on the edge of their seats. Barb Jones is not just an author; she is a master storyteller, redefining the boundaries of genre fiction.

www.thebloodprophecy.com

OTHER WORKS

blood prophecy series

queen's destiny
queen's enemy
queen's ascension

blood prophecy novellas

amber: birth of a queen
chloe: visions of the future
marcus: origins
machiel: stone of the damned
zaraquel: moral compass

blood prophecy: Dark prophecy series

rise of the hunter

heaven and hell series

BARB JONES

son of asmodeus
hell hounds

www.ingramcontent.com/pod-product-compliance
Lightning Source LLC
LaVergne TN
LVHW061544070526
838199LV00077B/6897